W9-BVZ-673

also by jennifer s. davis

HER KIND OF WANT

our former lives in art

jennifer s. davis

our former lives in art

(stories)

RANDOM HOUSE TRADE PAPERBACKS
NEW YORK

A Random House Trade Paperback Original

Published in the United States by Random House, an imprint of The Random House Publishing Group, a division of Random House, Inc., New York.

Random House Trade Paperbacks and colophon are trademarks of Random House, Inc.

ISBN 978-0-8129-7352-5

Some of the stories in this work have been previously published, in different form, as follows:
"Lovely Lily" in *Fiction,* "Detritus" in the *Indiana Review,* "Rapture" in *One Story,* "Pilgrimage in Georgia" in *The Oxford American,* "Giving Up the Ghost" in *The Paris Review,* "Our Former Lives in Art" in *Shenandoah,* and "Ava Bean" in *This Is Not Chick Lit: Original Stories by America's Best Women Writers* (New York: Random House, Inc., 2006).

LIBRARY OF CONGRESS CATALOGING-IN-PUBLICATION DATA
Davis, Jennifer S.
Our former lives in art: stories/Jennifer S. Davis.
p. cm.
Contents: Giving up the ghost—Lovely Lily—Ava Bean—Blue moon—Rapture—Pilgrimage in Georgia—Witnessing—Detritus—Our former lives in art.
ISBN-13: 978-0-8129-7352-5
ISBN-10: 0-8129-7352-6
1. Southern States—Social life and customs—Fiction.
I. Title.
PS3604.A96O94 2007   813'.6—dc22
2006049228

Printed in the United States of America on acid-free paper

www.atrandom.com

9 8 7 6 5 4 3 2 1

Text design by Laurie Jewell

FOR ERIC AND WILEY

Having been is also a kind of being,
and perhaps the surest kind.

—VIKTOR E. FRANKL

Man's Search for Meaning

contents

our former lives in art

giving up the ghost

"Look, Frank, trick-or-treaters," Carrie said, breaking the silence of the last half hour. "What are they doing all the way out here?"

"Here" was a country back road, eastern Alabama. Halloween, 1980.

"Those aren't trick-or-treaters," Frank said, easing the truck onto the sandy shoulder of the road. Up ahead, flipped on its side, half on the shoulder and half in the ditch, was a red-and-white-striped GMC Jimmy, one taillight blinking off and on, a maniacal, fluttering eye. Behind them, perhaps twenty feet, a knot of people huddled on the side of the road, not moving.

"Maybe we should drive on to the bait shop," Frank said. "Call the police from the pay phone." He had heard stories of people faking accidents in order to rob or rape unsuspecting Good Samaritans, and he couldn't help but wonder if this was it, the night a knife slid across his throat or, worse, Carrie's. The night everything was written out for them. The next morning, a work crew or a vagrant searching for aluminum cans would find their naked bodies on the side of the road, half-covered in wet pine needles, red clay.

"What's your problem?" Carrie snapped. She opened her door, slid from the truck. "They might be hurt. Don't just sit there."

The first thing he noticed when he opened his own door was the smell, hovering and sweet, like just bloomed honeysuckles. That mixed with gasoline and burnt rubber.

"Are y'all all right?" Carrie half yelled at the still unmoving knot behind them, but she stayed close to the truck.

A man, maybe forty, with pulpy, torn lips, finally loped over, extending his hand to Frank in a strange semblance of formality. He had hair cropped so short it had no color, light eyes to match. He wore an unbuttoned Hawaiian covered with little monkeys surfing. Behind him trailed a young woman and a small girl, just past toddler. Both of their faces were pretty banged up. They rushed toward Carrie as though they knew her, began clutching at her arms in a panic until Carrie awkwardly embraced them.

"You're the third car to come through here," the man said, grinding the heels of his boots into the grainy road. "No one else would stop. No one. Who could see two hurt girls and keep going?" He tugged a hand through his short hair, revealing a bloody forehead. "I just don't get it anymore, man. The big IT. You know what I mean?" He began crying, heaving gasps that horrified Frank. The man was shit-faced.

The woman had two-toned hair the yellow and copper of

poor white, and she wailed in response, pressed her face against Carrie's leather jacket. "I think they're more scared than hurt," Carrie said to no one in particular.

When the man reached for his wife, she pulled away. "My face, you idiot." Her fingers moved over her cheeks as if she could piece it back together. "I've told you a thousand times. A thousand. Slow. Down." The little girl clamped her eyes shut and didn't make a sound. She wore a striped leotard, one foot bare, the other in a tiny ballet slipper, the remnants of her Halloween costume, a bumblebee.

"That car flew out of fucking nowhere," the man said, suddenly angry. When he yelled, he sprayed blood instead of spit. He slammed a fist into his palm. "Nowhere." His wife and kid tried to burrow holes into Carrie with their faces; they seemed familiar with his anger.

"What car?" Frank said. He'd assumed that it was a one-car accident, a drunk man overcompensating for veering off the road, something anyone could do, including Frank, who'd had a beer or two himself that night.

The man pointed behind them, into the fringe of woods off the oncoming lane.

"You checked it out?" Frank asked. The man stared at his boots, shook his head no. The woman began whimpering, soft and wet.

Frank looked to where the man had pointed. There, some fifty feet away, as bright as the harvest moon that lit the night, was a yellow Camaro, its front crushed against an oak like crumpled paper. Glass and bits of metal glittered against the asphalt. There was no reasonable explanation for how he could have not noticed it until that moment, and he could hear the refrain Carrie had been saying lately: *You only see what you want to see, Frank. That's your problem.*

"You stay here," Frank said to Carrie. "Wave anyone down who passes. Ask if they have a CB radio."

It's strange, but on his walk over to the Camaro, this was what he thought: What a lovely night! How could anything so violent happen on such a night? It was still and pleasant, warm for late October, and if he tilted his head back, he could see nothing but blue-black and stars.

When he approached the car, he saw a teenage girl in a black leather dress, the bottom half of her body still in the driver's seat, her trunk slung out the opened door into the thick brush, her long blond hair tangled with debris, her face pale and still as the night. In such a dramatic position, she was bizarrely beautiful.

The girl looked dead, but to be sure, he knelt, placed his finger against her neck for a pulse. Her skin felt silky, soft. From the looks of her, she was the kind to pamper it, to spread creamy lotion over her neck, arms, elbows, chest. He held his finger there for a full minute before he felt a flicker, soft as eyelashes.

Frank cannot help but ask himself now, Should he have pulled her from the car? Would it have somehow made a difference, maybe lessen the loss of blood? What if he had pulled her from the car and jostled something vital, paralyzing her for life? Would he have received a phone call by now cursing him for his incompetence, blaming him for her wretched existence?

"Well?" Carrie yelled, impatient. "What's going on?"

"It's a girl," Frank said. "She's hurt. Bad." He was grateful that the Camaro and the trees blocked Carrie's view, grateful that she would not have to witness the girl's suffering.

At the sound of his voice, the girl's eyes popped open like an actress in a horror flick. "Hi," he said, as if they were meeting at a cocktail party. He took one of her hands in his. She wore a silver ring on each finger, gypsyish, a peculiarity he imagined some boy in her life found endearing. Her hand was cold, limp. He rubbed it as if he were warming a child's hand after a winter's day outside. He whispered all the things he thought you were supposed to say when someone was in anguish. Then he said nothing.

It's not quiet, death. Frank knows this now. Not like they tell you sometimes in books or on TV. Tales of people slipping from this world to the next like we slip in and out of clothes, just a change, another world, a light in a tunnel, perhaps, weightlessness, something like peace. The girl whispered things he never imagined himself whispering when he thought of his own death, something he had done compulsively in the year before he found her on that Halloween night in 1980. He imagined declarations, secrets revealed, illumination of spiritual truths. Instead, small things gurgled from her throat: the name of her kitten, the boy she had a crush on, the color of her bedroom. But it was not painless, the giving up of these details. She choked. She clawed. She wept.

"Whoa. That's bad. She alive?"

Frank looked up to see a red-bearded man in a camouflage jacket standing over him. The man's face was grooved, aged, the skin thick. Frank hadn't noticed anyone approach. The man reached for the girl, put his finger against her neck. "She's dead, sure enough. I already radioed in the accident, but I can't be around when the cops get here." The man turned, and without a backward glance, walked away.

All of it took maybe ten minutes.

After the man left, Frank could not seem to make himself walk back to the group he heard murmuring off in the distance. And then he thought, What if her parents had been notified? This was a small town. Many people had CB radios in their homes. What if her parents had heard the man call in the accident and recognized the description of the car? What if they were on their way to the scene right now? No parent should see a child like this.

He reached into the Camaro as best as he could and tugged at the hem of the girl's leather dress, attempting to cover the white expanse of her thin thighs. He picked the leaves from her golden hair and smoothed it from her forehead, easing it behind ears studded with silver crosses, then decided that her hair would look better falling in soft waves around her face, so he arranged it that way. He licked his fingers, wiped the mud and streaks of blood from her cheeks, and marveled that there was hardly a scratch on her face, that the only visible injury appeared to be to her chest; and before he could stop himself, he reached for her wound, the exact point where the steering wheel had hit, and put his hand against her heart, perhaps not believing it could stop so easily.

She wore a gold locket, a delicate, heart-shaped thing, hard under his fingers, still warm with her body heat. He stared at it for a moment, flipping it over and over in his hand like a worry stone, studied the inscription on the back: *On your sweet sixteen, Forever our baby girl.* Still kneeling, he unhooked the locket from around her neck and wedged it into his pocket, wiping her blood on his jeans.

When Frank thinks of this moment now, he remembers that he saw everything by the light of the moon. But he worries that he might have made parts of it up, and it's a thing like getting something wrong that haunts him, not ever truly knowing what's real and what's not.

• • •

Later, after they'd waited with the couple and their daughter for the ambulance and answered all the questions for the police, Frank and Carrie finally started the drive to their cabin for what they'd hoped would be a few days of quiet.

"You know what makes me sick?" Carrie said. "That drunk might as well have put a gun to that teenager's head and shot her. And more than likely, nothing will happen to him."

It was true. Back then, no one paid much attention to drunk drivers. Everyone carried coolers on their floorboards, wrapped beer cans in fake Coke covers as disguises. Frank had done it a hundred times, and he would do it again, although he told himself differently that night.

"And who would drive drunk with a beautiful little girl in the car?" Carrie said. "What kind of father would do that? What kind? They don't deserve that little girl."

Frank turned on the radio so he wouldn't have to talk or think. An old country ballad about a man who drinks a woman up to a ten in a honky-tonk.

"You know what else?" Carrie said a few minutes later, turning down the radio. Her face shone in the moon's glare. She was trying not to cry, something Frank wished he hadn't noticed, because now he would have to deal with it, and he didn't know how. Her voice lowered in a way that let Frank know she expected absolution. "I didn't really want to touch that girl and woman because they were all covered in blood and I have on my new leather blazer. I didn't want them to ruin it." She began sobbing, pulling at her blazer, slapping her chest like a madwoman. "Can you believe that? What kind of person thinks that kind of thing?"

Then later, "Frank? Why does life have to be so relentlessly cyclical? Why can't we move in some other direction? Why?"

• • •

That Saturday at the cabin, Frank and Carrie sunbathed naked on their front porch, skinny-dipped in the chilly waters of the lake. They drank screwdrivers and daiquiris, danced to Pink Floyd and Lynyrd Skynyrd, and made love on the deck, on the boat, on the picnic table, anywhere that prohibited honest intimacy.

Neither Carrie nor Frank mentioned the accident, but it was there, always, the understanding of the brevity of things, the knowledge that there would be no eternity of lovemaking, of dancing drunkenly on the front porch. To Frank, it felt like a lie, this performance of carefree love, so he laughed the loudest, danced the longest, and reached for Carrie's body as soon as his pulse slowed from their previous bout of lovemaking, telling himself there was only this, the here and now: Carrie's mouth, Carrie's thrumming heart.

Saturday evening, the night was unseasonably warm, the low-slung moon covered in clouds, and still half-drunk from sun and booze, they decided to grill steaks. Carrie wore only a bathrobe. She sat in a patio chair sipping a glass of wine, her heels cocked on the porch railing so that her satin robe spilled open. Her long legs, her breasts, the stretch of her neck, incandescent in the moonlight. Sitting as she was, staring into the distance, she seemed to Frank inaccessible and far away, a stranger, someone else's wife, and he couldn't quite remember how they'd gotten here, to this porch in Alabama, grilling steaks.

Carrie lit a cigarette, blew a delicate stream of smoke. "I'm not ovulating, you know. I just wanted you to know that. All the sex—it was just that. No ulterior motives." She turned to him where he stood over the grill, nervously flipping the steaks from one side to the other, and waited.

"That's good," he said. "I appreciate that. You telling me." But even as he said it, he worried that it wouldn't be enough, that nothing he said would ever be enough again.

Carrie had miscarried at seven months, a baby haphazardly conceived one drunken night, a pregnancy that had launched their marriage into unexpected, terrifying territory. Carrie had been devastated by the loss. Partially, Frank suspected, because she had been slightly relieved when she miscarried and was horrified by her response.

After the funeral, things got ugly. They named the baby Mary Grace, and Carrie talked about her constantly, as though if she referenced Mary Grace enough, she could create a history for their daughter. The doctor gave Carrie pills to dry up her milk, but she wouldn't take them, and for a week or so there were bottles and cans and bowls of pumped breast milk everywhere, the smell sour and intolerable. Carrie walked around the house in the dirty pink pajamas, her belly rounded, her hands cupped around her breasts. Watching her sit in the empty nursery in his grandmother's rocking chair, a suction cup on her breast, her rocking and staring and crying, made Frank fist-through-the-wall angry. Not at Carrie, but at something he couldn't put a name to, which made it even worse for her because she couldn't tell the difference.

When the doctor gave them the thumbs-up a year ago, Carrie refused to discuss the possibility that maybe a baby was not the best thing with Frank just starting a new landscaping business. Instead, as if having a family had always been the plan, the miscarriage merely an obstacle, she began trying with the discipline of a soldier to get pregnant, and failed, and therefore was failing life in general, and because of this failure, resenting Frank. Frank, who had seemed untouched by the miscarriage, who had returned to work the next day, where he met with a carefully casual rich man in khakis to talk about how to landscape his summer home's front yard, how to make it a work of art.

But Carrie was mellow tonight, introspective and thoughtful, and she did not attack Frank, just sat and smoked and watched the cloud-muted moon heft itself into the vault of the sky.

"Why don't you grab a plate?" Frank asked. "I think these are almost ready." He wore his *Kiss the Cook* apron, big red lips seared across his abdomen. He puckered his own mouth at Carrie, and she waved her hand at him to stop.

"Do you wonder about her?" Carried asked, not moving toward the kitchen. She crushed out her cigarette, fumbled with the pack, then pulled out another and lit it. "Who she was? What she was like?"

"The baby?" Frank asked, flipping the steaks again. "Sure," he said, which was only a half lie, because he had thought about it after the baby had died. In fact, he was so concerned by his detached response when Carrie had called him at work and told him that the baby had no heartbeat, that he'd forced himself to sit in the hospital waiting room and visualize it, his dead child floating in his wife's belly. The exact moment the baby's heart stopped, where he and Carrie might have been—watching *Alien* at the theater, eating hamburgers at the Dairy Queen. But for the most part, the sorrow always felt manufactured and remote.

"No," Carrie snapped. "The girl from last night."

Frank felt dizzy again, the same light-headed feeling he'd had kneeling over the girl's body. "Vivian," he said softly. "She said her name was Vivian."

"Well?"

"Well what?"

"What did she say? She told you her name. She must have said something else." Carrie fumbled with her robe, tugging it over her breasts. She wore the studied expression of indifference of a woman trying not to look too interested in information that she was uncertain she had any right to know. It reminded Frank of the one time he had cheated on her in college—her slowly emerging questions, her masochistic desire to learn every detail, location, position, what was whispered during and after, if he had held the woman in the afterglow, shared a late night snack, a glass of water. Frank suspected that for Carrie, the sex wasn't as much of a betrayal as the possibility that he'd given something of himself to another, something he'd been holding back from her.

What he hadn't told Carrie: He and the other woman, a girl from class he'd run into at a local bar, stayed up all night singing Bob Dylan songs and drinking shots of tequila; just before dawn they'd made love again, then driven over to the Theta Chi house and lobbed golf balls at the windows because the girl's ex-boyfriend lived there and he was an asshole; later, they'd eaten breakfast at the Waffle House. The girl wore a T-shirt Carrie had left over at his apartment. This had excited him somehow, watching the girl nibble on her biscuit and talk about her ex while wearing Carrie's shirt, *It's All a Matter of Perspective* printed across her breasts.

"That was it," Frank said. "Just her name." He waved the fork like a wand, grinned. "Voilà! Done. Now where's that plate?"

"I'm not hungry," Carrie said. She lowered her legs from the railing and stood up, drained the last of her wine, snatched the pack of cigarettes, and went into the house, turning off the kitchen and porch lights, leaving Frank standing in the dark.

• • •

The Tuesday after the accident, Frank asked his secretary to cancel his appointments and headed out for Alexander City, where he parked his truck across the street from the graveyard. He counted over a hundred mourners in attendance and tried to match the names he'd read in the obituary to faces. Lois Brown, the mother, wore hot pink. William Brown, the father, wore a navy suit and an old Vegas-style hat. The sister, a plump, red-faced preadolescent, threw a lily on the casket, then wailed, very theatrical. The brother looked like every other pissed-off teenager. They sang "Amazing Grace," "Peace in the Valley," and "Just as I Am." The preacher offered dozens of platitudes, empty words Frank guessed Vivian would have hated.

About an hour after the cemetery cleared, Frank finally got out of his truck and walked on the tender grass path, covered in constellations of fresh red clay footprints, to the burial site. A mound of flowers curved over Vivian's grave. There were dozens of stuffed animals holding hearts in their various paws, photos of her with her friends, and handwritten letters in loopy script. Frank kept one. *Dear Viv, I know we grew apart this year because of me getting the cheerleading spot and stuff, but I thought you were awesome and you should've made the squad and I just cannot believe you died. Ms. Mise's first period class won't be the same without you. BFF, Penelope.*

Vivian didn't have a tombstone yet, just a tiny metal marker, 3356L. They'd placed her under a huge oak, and Frank thought it nice. A girl who wore jewelry and lotion and soft leather dresses would appreciate a thing of beauty.

"Man, she was one crazy chick," said a voice from behind him. "But you had to love her. You couldn't not love her."

Frank turned to see a slight young man, eighteen at most, his body pulled long and lean from nervousness, dark hair to his bony shoulder blades, a concert T-shirt with a band's name Frank didn't recognize.

"Sure," Frank said, annoyed at the intrusion. But he couldn't help but wonder why this boy was here now, hiding like him from the rest of the mourners, willing to talk to a stranger about a girl he seemingly loved. Then he smelled the alcohol. Saw the boy sway, fight to stand straight.

The teenager collapsed to his knees beside Frank, growled, cupped a handful of red dirt from near the grave, slung it across the graveyard, a gesture that came off more as an appropriation of grief than actual emotion. Most of the dirt ended up on Frank's face.

"We were supposed to be on a date," the boy said, his dark eyes watering. "We were supposed to be together, but I was a fucking idiot and started some shit and now look." He tapped a Marlboro out of a crushed pack and lit it, sucking hard. He pulled a Budweiser from his jacket pocket, cracked it open, took a long drink, then wiped his mouth with the back of his hand.

"You want a beer?" he said. "I got a whole case in my car."

"I found her," Frank said softly. "At the wreck. I found her there."

"Yeah?"

"Yeah," Frank said. "But I knew her before then." The last part slipped out, and strangely, felt true enough. Besides, perhaps he knew Vivian better than anyone. Perhaps what she'd offered him the night she died was the core of herself, what she wanted left behind. It made sense, really, and once Frank thought it, it became true.

"What's your name?" the boy asked, suspicious. He stood up, towered.

"Frank. Frank King."

"She never mentioned a Frank. And the papers said a stranger found her."

"What do the papers know?"

"Where'd you meet?" the kid said.

Frank realized that to this boy, he must seem old, an impossibility in Vivian's world, and for some reason this made him angry or sad or lonely.

"Out," he said. "We talked about things. Lots of things."

"You fuck her?" the boy said, his voice rising. "Because if you fucked her, I'm going to need to know, you know?"

"It wasn't like that," Frank said.

The kid looked soft for a second, vulnerable. Then, "Can you show me where it happened? You know, where she died?"

They walked in silence to the boy's beat-up Volvo, probably his mother's old car pool hand-me-down, and Frank waited while the kid unlocked his trunk, pulled out a case of Budweiser.

The boy finally offered a name when he slid with his case of beer into Frank's truck, immediately flipping the radio stations. Keith.

"Nice stereo," Keith said. "I'm saving up for some twelve-inch woofers myself. I want people to hear me coming." Frank thought it might be a good idea for the world at large to have a warning of Keith's arrival.

"You mind if we make a detour?" Frank said, swinging the truck in front of the pay phone at the gas station a few blocks from the graveyard. He pulled the keys from the ignition, just in case Keith was the kind of person he suspected he was.

Keith shrugged. "I got a lifetime," he said, unsmiling.

• • •

Lois Brown greeted Frank at the door in a hot pink jumpsuit, which she smoothed over her hips compulsively. There were a few people still milling around from the funeral in the kitchen, probably freezing casseroles and hams and cakes. Kids screamed from somewhere. When Frank called from the gas station to see if Mrs. Brown wanted to meet with him, she told him to come right over. Keith opted to wait in the car. Bad blood, he'd said.

"It drove Vivian crazy," Mrs. Brown said, fluttering her hand at nothing in particular. "All the pink." She was seated across from Frank in the formal living room. The floor was pink marble, the décor as ornate as a French palace. The rest of the enormous house, at least what Frank had seen, had been decorated in tasteful neutrals.

"This was the only room William would let me have my way with," Mrs. Brown explained. She smiled sadly. The skin beneath her eyes was the color of an old bruise. She looked to be heavily medicated. "Pink. It's just my thing."

"It's very nice." If Mrs. Brown heard him, she gave no indication.

"My whole life I was in love with the South," she continued. "I was raised in Connecticut, but I never felt at home there." She twirled a lock of blond hair, thin as cirrus clouds. She had an angry red sore at the base of her thumb. "I saw *Gone With the Wind* a thousand times. At least." She sighed. "When the Tarleton twins died in the war, God, I cried." Without warning, she got down on her little pink knees, started clawing in the Oriental carpet, held up a fake handful of dirt, said in a deadpan, lackluster voice, "As God is my witness."

Mr. Brown stuck his balding head in the door. "Everything okay in here?" He had the veranda porch accent of old money.

Mrs. Brown waved him away. "He hates it when I do that,"

she said, climbing back on the couch, completely demure. "That's where Vivian got her name, the movie." She smoothed her hands repeatedly over her hips and thighs, and Frank tried to imagine the Vivian he knew living in this house with this woman.

"Is Mr. Brown joining us?" Frank asked.

"Emotion gives him the hives." She snorted. "Cool as a cucumber. Cold as ice."

Frank smiled. Fingered a pink embroidered flower on the sofa pillow.

"They were just babies," she said. "Just babies."

"Who?" Frank said, confused.

"The Tarleton twins," she said. "So sad." She shook her head as if remembering long-ago lost loves. "Everybody at home laughed at me, said all I'd find down here were rednecks and racists, but I thought it was magical. Then some white-trash drunk runs down my daughter, and no one is going to do a damn thing about it. They think I don't know, but I saw the Jimmy. I went to the wreck yard. I saw the beer cans."

She stood up, began pumping around the room in her hot pink stilettos, gouging at the sore place on her hand. Then Mrs. Brown was in front of Frank, kneeling, her twitching hands on his knees. "What did she say about me?" Mrs. Brown asked. "Was she in pain?" Mrs. Brown asked. "Did she pray?" Mrs. Brown asked.

Frank lied when necessary, when the truth would have been too harsh, but for the most part he told her everything he could remember, down to the turn of Vivian's body, the way she squeezed his hand right before she went. When he finished, he felt strangely exhilarated, as if he had run a great distance. But Vivian's mother appeared more devastated than comforted by what he'd told her, and he thought, How stupid. Stupid Frank. He'd never get it right.

"Mrs. Brown?" he said, his hands covering hers on his knees. "Would you mind if I saw her room? I feel close to her, somehow, you know?"

Vivian's room was painted a deep purple, the bedspread black velvet. Band posters papered the walls, AC/DC, Black Sabbath, Pink Floyd. A delicate Oriental umbrella hung upside down from the ceiling. The room smelled thick, like cigarette smoke and too many perfume samples from fashion magazines.

Mrs. Brown sat down delicately on the bed; her face buckled. "This is the first time I've been able to come in here since we heard," she said. She waved a hand at the walls. "Eggplant. I always hated this room. What teenage girl wants an eggplant-and-black bedroom?" Her pink shoulders began quaking.

Frank experienced a sudden, terrifying desire, saw an image of him pressing his mouth against Mrs. Brown's cool white neck, of taking those fidgeting fingers into his mouth and sucking them, one by one, of laying her gently down on that black velvet spread and loving her in a way he suspected she had not been loved in some time. At least he could give her that.

But of course, he only sat beside her, put his hand on hers, then removed it. They rested there for a while like old friends, comfortable in their separate silences, their separate grief.

● ● ●

"Crazier than her daughter, huh?" Keith said when Frank got back to the truck. Keith had his feet hanging out of the rolled-down window, his seat reclined as far back as it would go. "Me and Mrs. B, there ain't no love lost there."

They started out for the wreck site, almost fifteen miles outside of town. No one knew why Vivian was driving on such a secluded road by herself that night.

"It was because of me. She was mad at me," Keith insisted, digging in his coat. "Mind if I smoke?"

"You together long?" Frank asked.

"Off and on," Keith said, hacking. He failed to mention that what he was smoking was dope. "You want a hit?" He offered the joint to Frank.

Half-stoned. The drive felt endless. The road wound around the lake, glimpses of the sun reflecting off the water as blindingly sharp as opening a bar door to morning after an all-night binge.

"So did y'all have plans?" Frank asked. "You and Vivian. It's good to have a plan." Frank was stoned.

"Sure," Keith said. "We had plans. Everyone has plans. You got tweezers or something? This thing's getting hot." Frank motioned at the glove compartment, and Keith fished around until he found one of Carrie's barrettes and fastened it onto the end of the joint, then lifted the makeshift roach clip for Frank's approval. "Like Bond, dude, 007. You make do with what you've got."

Frank laughed, reached for the roach.

"Prom," Keith said, releasing a mouthful of captive smoke. "We were going to prom together in April. Viv was going to wear a tux. She liked to stir things up. And then maybe community college for a year before transferring up to Tuscaloosa. Get an apartment. Get married. She wanted to study psychology.

Wanted to work with fucked-up kids with fucked-up parents. Viv was cool that way. Always thinking about kids and animals and bullshit. I mean, you met her parents. It ain't hard to figure out why."

Frank knew Vivian and Keith would have never attended college together, that Keith, a reckless country boy who would end up at the mill or behind a gas station counter, was the kind of high school love always better left behind, and girls like Vivian understood this intuitively. There would have been no apartment, no marriage. Maybe the prom, maybe afterward an evening of drunken promises whispered in a room in the tiny motel near town where teenage lovers have shared details of unforgeable, improbable dreams for decades. And then Vivian would have left to attend school, and with her parents' money, not at some community college. And maybe she would have written Keith a few times, called him drunk after a party or her first college heartbreak, told him that she missed him, that she wished he were there. But that wouldn't have been true, exactly. Frank wanted to tell Keith all of this, wanted to tell the boy that growing to an age where you understand plans are almost useless things is a kind of death in itself; but he lacked the courage or the cruelty to do it.

"I was going to be a musician, like Dylan or Garcia," Frank said instead. "My wife wanted to be a painter. Abstract. Picasso-like. Fragmentation and alienation. She was good. We were going to travel around the world. Then maybe, around forty, adopt a bunch of orphans from China or Africa."

He grabbed a beer from Keith's stash on the floorboard, cracked it open, and took a long swallow, his mouth and throat parched from the dope. Then he thought of Vivian and handed his beer to Keith.

"But now I design yards for rich fuckers on the lake. Build piers and porches for extra cash. And Carrie does portraits of family pets. You see what I'm trying to tell you?"

"I hate Dylan," Keith said. "And the Dead. All that hopeful, handholding shit. They don't get it, you know what I mean?"

He turned up the radio. Black Sabbath's "Wicked World" blared.

The world today has such a wicked face . . .

"This," Keith said, banging his head. "This is all there is."

Frank turned down the radio, irritated. Irritated that Vivian would have wasted her time on this boy, a loser any girl with good sense would avoid.

A few minutes later, Frank eased off the shoulder at the same spot from Halloween. He'd stopped by the accident several times since it had happened, examined every piece of grass, every pinecone, knelt where he had knelt beside Vivian. And then he'd wept, replaying that night, pressing Vivian's locket against his chest, which he'd worn under his clothes since he'd read her obituary on Sunday.

"Where?" Keith said. Frank pointed into the fringe of trees where a scattering of flowers had been left. The Camaro's skid marks were still visible.

Frank sat in the truck, watched Keith in the rearview mirror as he loped long-legged down the road behind him. The boy stood still in the road for a few moments, his dark hair shimmering like the sun-hammered asphalt.

Keith raised his hands to the sky, then walked to the shoulder where Vivian's car left the pavement, crouched, took something shiny from his boot, and began sawing at his hair with it. By the time Frank realized he had a knife, Keith was whipping the blade against his left forearm.

Frank was out of the truck, had the boy's arms pulled behind his back, his cheek smashed into the ground. "Shhh," Frank said to soothe him. "It's not worth it. Trust me, it's not." He placed his own cheek against Keith's, made a sound something like humming and exhaling.

"Have you fucking lost your mind, man?" Keith said, untangling himself. Frank's chest ached; spittle ran down his chin. Keith had a knife caked with blood and dirt in one hand, a handful of his hair in the other.

"I'm mourning," he said. "It's a Native American tradition." He held out his bony arms. The cuts he'd made were shallow, superficial. "The scars remind the living of the dead." He smiled, his teeth already yellowing. "I'm part Cherokee, and it's a Cheyenne tradition, but hell, like I care. Viv thought it was romantic."

Frank sat in the dirt and watched while Keith danced around the roadside and made Indian-ish sounds.

"This is hard-core, huh?" Keith said to Frank when he'd finished the dance. Then he kissed his shorn hair, tossed it in the air, and laughed as it rained around them in black streams.

• • •

Frank read about a man once in the tabloids, a man who recorded things, wrote down every minute of his life for the last thirty years. He knew that he ate three-quarters of a can of tomato soup on February 4, 1956, at 12:31 p.m., that he opened the can at 12:22, turned on the oven at 12:23, washed his bowl and pan at 12:48. At first it was just a hobby, but it didn't take long for him to become obsessed, and then he grew disoriented if things happened too quickly to write down, until finally, he recorded every second of his day. He said he recorded his life to make sure that he'd lived one, to offer evidence to himself and to the world. He'd explained in the interview that by the time he became an old man, he could no longer leave the house. Volunteers had to bring him food, do his shopping, answer his phone, because the doing prohibited the recording, so others lived his life for him. At the end of the interview, the man had been frantic, fearful that he wouldn't be able to recapture everything that had occurred in the previous hours.

Frank told the story of this man to Carrie that Tuesday night in bed, the day of Vivian Leigh Brown's funeral. He asked her what she thought about it.

"Details," he said. "The particulars. It's all we have, all that makes us who we are, you know?"

How could a person just not *be* anymore? That's what Carrie had asked after the baby died. That, and if she had done something wrong. Chosen a poor doctor, a second-rate hospital. Skimped on her vitamins. Snuck one too many sips of wine. What if? she'd said. What if? When Frank couldn't offer a satisfactory answer, she'd taken it as condemnation.

"I peaked," she said, ignoring him. "My temperature peaked and I called the office and you weren't there." She'd dressed up for him, a white frilly negligee, a tornado of wispy brown hair. Ovulation.

"I know what you are up to, why you've been so distant these past months," Carrie said. She grabbed his chin with her shaking hands. Made him look into her eyes until he lost focus and her face became one large, blurry, faraway accusatory pupil. "I wasn't sure," she said, letting go of his face. "But I am now."

She began sniffling, rubbing at her face, and it hit Frank like a punch, what she thought. And maybe he had cheated on her in a way. How much easier it is, Frank thought, to give to strangers what is too difficult to give to the ones who have witnessed our small, wretched failures. So perhaps he deserved this, Carrie's anger, whatever retribution would follow. Maybe a new kind of anger was what they needed, a perverse catalyst for change.

"And I've decided to get better. I can. And if you've decided that we're getting a divorce, you can undecide. Now. So give me the locket. Don't think I don't know about it."

Frank unlatched Vivian's locket, warm from his skin, and dangled it in front of Carrie. If Carrie looked inside, she'd find the face of a young Vivian, front teeth missing, her hair in uneven braids, and a small snippet of blond hair, probably from Vivian's first haircut. Carrie snatched it from his hand, stuck it in her bedside table, then turned her back to Frank. She opened a book and began reading. And things were different between them. Just like that.

"We won't mention it again," she said, flipping the page. "But know I know."

When Carrie fell asleep, soft and peacefully, as if this day were any other, Frank watched her, his miraculous wife. The breathing in and out, her chest rising and falling. He put his hand over her mouth, her breath warm in his palm, placed his lips against hers, opened them slightly, inhaled.

There's an old superstition Frank's grandmother told him as a boy. When a person dies, you have to make sure the mouth stays open at the exact moment of death so the spirit can escape the body, and that soft sigh you hear when someone breathes her last, that's the sigh of abandon, departure. After Vivian Leigh Brown died, he worried he'd inhaled a bit of her from that bubbling mouth into him, if maybe that was why he couldn't let go, couldn't stop feeling the soft shudder of her body when it no longer became hers. And he worried about Mary Grace after she'd died, never opening her mouth, never taking a breath. He worried she'd be trapped in that impossibly tiny corpse—or worse, in Carrie, in the core of her, fluttering there broken, until a part of Carrie died, too. Perhaps the last part that loved him.

Carrie swatted at him in her sleep, curled onto her side. And suddenly, Frank wanted nothing more than to hold his wife's sleeping body, so he tucked his knees into hers, pressed his face into her back. He told himself to remember: the warmth and sharpness of Carrie's shoulder blade against his cheek, her smell, yeasty and sweet; the fading of an ambulance's siren as it traveled down the county road; the painting of a half-finished yellow canary resting on an easel by the open window; the feeling that for a brief, quiet moment, Frank was exactly where he should be.

lovely lily

When Lily enters the community center, an elderly woman in a mean green jumpsuit smiles from behind a card table serving as a reception desk. "Howdy," she says. "You here for the program?" The pamphlets fanned across the table read "Love Knows No Age."

"No," Lily says, "for the bingo."

The woman, who Lily figures is old enough to be dead several times over, laughs too hard. She seems unimpressed by Lily's shaved head, her piercings, her white-powdered skin, her outfit and general mood: black.

Lily's mother, who drove Lily to the community center to make sure she actually went, explained during the ride that this is a new program that pairs up troubled teens with isolated retired people. Last month it had been therapeutic dancing. The month before, a class on expressing your rage through the didgeridoo.

"You give them life," she'd said when she dropped

Lily off, "and they give you advice on how to live yours." She'd read the brochure.

"Do you hate me for some reason?" Lily had said.

"What's your name?" the lady asks.

"Queen of the Dark," Lily answers.

"I'm Miss Lolita."

"Sounds like a stripper's name," Lily says. Lolita does a little shuffling shimmy, her long, glittering earrings dancing against the folds of her neck, then winks, as if that just might be the case.

If Jessica were alive and this were a normal day, she and Lily would be making bubble-letter banners for the basketball team. KILL THOSE TIGERS. GO WILDCATS GO! Or perhaps they would be trying on clothes at Express, checking out the season's sexy lace-up boots, the kind their parents would never let them wear. They'd sleep over at Jessica's house because her parents were rarely home. They'd sneak X-rated movies and weed from the old army trunk her father kept in his closet, giggling, happily stoned, at the fake-chested porn stars, their bodies full of startled, puckered O's.

"Here we go," Lolita says, slapping a sticker name tag on Lily's chest that announces, "Hello, My Name Is Queenie." "Looks like you're our guinea pig. First kid in the program."

Lolita nods toward a bent man wearing a wife beater who stands under a stream of dusty spring light in the corner of the room. A jaunty fedora perches on his head, and he clutches a free weight in each hand, the small kind Lily's mother uses when she does her old Jane Fonda tapes. His arms are spastic from the exertion. He's strapped to an oxygen tank, the thin tubes snaking up his nostrils. Behind him hang posters advertising the benefits of staying young, pandering vitamins and exercise equipment. A lush grapefruit dances in a top hat, its gloved hand twirling a cane made out of celery.

"You get Alfred," Lolita says. Besides Lily and Lolita, he is the only other person in the room.

"What am I supposed to do with him?"

"Talk about things." The way Lolita says "things" makes Lily nervous, because she knows that means how she feels about Jessica and her grades and why she wears black lipstick and where she goes after school when she doesn't come home on time, all the things her parents and teachers and therapist want her to talk about.

"This will help get the conversation started." Lolita shoves a pamphlet into Lily's hand.

When Lily walks over to Alfred, he eyes her appreciatively, the way the icky old men in the mall lounging on benches while their wives shopped used to watch her and Jessica.

She stops a few feet away from him and points at her name tag.

"You mute, Queenie?" he says, tossing his weights on an exercise pad. " 'Cause that might pose a challenge."

"Are you some kind of pervert?" she says. "Because I know enough of those already."

"What dulcet tones. You do speak."

"Huh?" Lily says. She crosses her arms protectively over her chest, although her men's suit jacket and tight sports bra hide any suggestion of breasts.

"You're safe," Alfred says, nodding toward her arms. "I'm too sick to be a pervert." He doesn't smile when he says it.

Lily follows Alfred to a corner of the room where a series of fold-up chairs are set up in a semicircle. He moves slowly, painfully, pausing every few steps to catch his breath, his oxygen tank dragging behind him. He exhales heavily when he sits down, as if someone has punched him. Lily leaves an empty chair between them. They stare at each other in silence, their hands folded in their laps.

"I'm not so good with people," Alfred says apologetically. "I kind of got suckered into this by Lolita. She brings me meals sometimes when I can't get out. It was either do this or have her drive me plumb mad." He waves at the old woman at the table, and she waves back wildly before offering a thumbs-up sign. Lily cringes at the enthusiasm. What a freak, she thinks. Then, if this was what it's like to get old, she doesn't know if she'll bother.

"We're supposed to answer the questions in the pamphlet," Lily says, trying not to notice the blooms of bruises on the thin skin of Alfred's wasted arms.

"Fire away." A thick, puckered scar cuts a path from Alfred's eyebrow to his cheekbone, and one of his eyelids droops. When he tries to meet her eyes with his, he looks drunk or deranged or both.

Lily focuses on the pamphlet, begins reading in a monotone. "What do you love most?" At first, they both offer vague answers. Peace. "What is peace to you?" Love. When Lily asks the last question, what he hopes to get out of the program, Alfred grins and says that he hopes to pick up some young women. He wears a poker face, wizened and tinged gray, his one good eye as emotionless as still water.

"I'm only half-serious," he says finally. "I haven't exactly made a lot of friends in my life. It gets lonely, dying."

"What did you do before you got sick?"

"I reckon the same that I do now," he says. "Sit at home and wish I'd done something different. What do you do?"

"The same thing," Lily says, and when she says it, Alfred nods sympathetically, as though she's a normal person giving a normal answer, and before she knows it, she's telling him about Catalyst.

"It's a school for emotional 'tards. They put me there this year because I failed eleventh grade. Because I'm unstable, whatever that means. Apparently, I'm not a *happy* person."

At Catalyst, they don't take normal high school classes. The school has its own name and sign as if it's official, but basically Catalyst consists of a donated double-wide trailer plopped in a patch of weeds behind the regular high school's gym. Even so, all the students are assured they will graduate on schedule and go to college, a place Lily, once an honor roll student, never really thinks about anymore. When her parents ask about her future plans, she answers, Harvard, stone-faced. When her mother says don't be a smart aleck, Lily asks why the idea of her attending Harvard is so funny. "Please, Lily," her mother says. Which means, *What's wrong with you?* Which means, *I can't do this anymore.*

Instead of regular classes, Catalyst offers special seminars on photography or botany, a session of all things Renaissance, anything to keep the students diverted, upbeat. Once the students threw a medieval banquet where they wore obnoxious, overpriced rental costumes and ate out of a trough, then watched a video of reenactors jousting on horses. Pinkie, the resident anorexic, sat on her hands so she wouldn't be tempted to touch the food. There's always the danger that one of them will be adversely affected by the content of the special seminars, and on any given day, Catalyst can seem more like a psych ward than a school.

"Sounds like a retirement home," Alfred says, and Lily laughs before she can stop herself.

"I grew up on a boat," Alfred says. "My parents were radicals of sorts. When I got interested in something, my dad handed me a book and told me to figure it out. Said that education was the individual's responsibility. It made for interesting learning but didn't do much for my social skills, you know?"

"A boat." Lily sighs. "I bet you had a bitchin' tan." She touches the pale skin of her cheek, stiff with powder. If she tries really hard, she can see Jessica exactly as she looked the last day of summer break before she died. She's wearing white cotton underwear and a pink lace bra, and she's lying in her backyard on a faded Cinderella beach towel she got on a trip to Disney World when she was ten. A *Cosmo* is spread across her bronzed chest, and she's saying something while laughing, although Lily can no longer make out the words.

"What do you expect out of the program?" Alfred says.

"Not much."

"Toothsome," Alfred says. "Whether you hide yourself or not."

Lily scowls at him, uncertain if he just insulted her, says, "I had braces for like umpteen years."

"No," Alfred says, leaning toward her. "It's my word of the day. Toothsome. I got me one of those Word of the Day calendars. That way I know at least I'm learning something new, that I ain't wasting what I got left. It means pleasant or attractive. So see," he says, placing a shaky hand on her arm, "you learned something. You already got more than you expected."

"Whatever," Lily says. Under Alfred's intent gaze, she feels a pang for the loss of her long hair, which she shaved to piss off her mother, which worked brilliantly, even though Lily never really considered the fact that she'd actually be bald far after her mother freaked out. Now she wishes she could toss her hair in front of her face and disappear.

"You hungry?" Alfred says. "We could blow this joint and go to the mall for some lunch. Surely you like the mall. Isn't that a given for a girl, even an angry one?"

"But it's like nine o'clock," Lily says. Unless forced to go to school, which is a joke anyway, Lily prefers not to wake before noon. Then she watches soap operas for a few hours until Oprah comes on. Then MTV until reruns of *Law & Order* kick in. If she remembers to eat, it's usually already dark outside.

"It's lunchtime somewhere," Alfred says.

Lily is about to say no, *fuck you,* when she thinks of her mother, who at this moment is probably dancing to her exercise tapes in the den, thinking about what a resourceful mother she is. She would kill Lily for going off with a strange man.

"Sure," Lily says. "I can do the mall."

• • •

On the ride over, Alfred tells Lily that he's not exactly retirement age. In fact, he's only fifty-one. He just looks like a much older man because he's sucked dry as a husk from emphysema. He used to be a welder but isn't much use to anyone anymore. He's divorced with a grown kid he hasn't seen in years. He likes

Johnny Cash and George Jones, singers Lily has never heard of, and misses eating tamales, which give him indigestion now because of his medication.

Lily only half listens. Instead, she stares out the window, watches the sun filter by, the generic buildings of their town dappled with light so that they almost shimmer, like a mirage. Lately, Lily feels as if she's fading. As if there is some other girl, a stranger, sitting in the passenger seat next to a dying man talking about boats, and she can hear him, see his mouth form the words out of the corner of her eye, and she can feel the heat from the sun-soaked side console under her arm, the air-conditioning blowing in her face, but she's not there. Not really.

"One of the perks," Alfred says when he pulls into a handicapped space in the mall parking lot. "You got to make the best of a bad situation." He tips his hat at her and raises one eyebrow. Lily wonders if the other one works.

It takes Alfred several minutes to get out of the car and arrange his tank, then several more to make it to the doors of the mall. Before he enters, he pulls out a pair of sunglasses and puts them on. This seems strange to Lily, since he didn't wear them in the car. They're huge, covering half his face, and the people loitering in the doorway scatter out of his path like he's blind.

"I think you're safe from the sun," Lily says. "You can lose the shades."

"The eye freaks people out. This way I look like a star, like Bocephus. Not like a mutant."

"Who?" A preppie boy Lily recognizes from her old school eyes Alfred's tank, Lily's oversized zoot suit and black combat boots. He doesn't even try to hide his stare. Lily flips him the finger.

"You don't know nothing, do you." Alfred begins singing in his raspy voice, "All my rowdy friends done settled down . . ." but he runs out of breath after one line. He seems to find this hilarious, and Lily understands why Alfred might not have many friends. That possibly, he's a little insane. Lily decides that she likes him.

"This tank throws me off," Alfred says. "You mind if I hold your hand for balance? It's been a long time since I held a pretty girl's hand."

Lily isn't so sure, but they are in the mall, and there isn't much harm he could do in a public place. She slips her hand into his cold dry one, and she is surprised by how natural it feels. It is the first time in a long time she remembers being comfortable when someone touched her.

Alfred wants to exercise before they eat, and none of the lunch places are open yet, so they walk hand in hand through Parisian's and Claire's Boutique, Alfred walking so slowly that Lily almost trips over her feet trying to take small steps. Alfred offers to buy her something, a pair of earrings, a lipstick, keeps holding up blouses and skirts he thinks might look good on her, tacky things with sequins or floral prints. Lily can think of nothing she wants. Girls her age walk by with armloads of clothes, chattering in sharp, silly voices.

"You got any friends?" Alfred says, admiring the girls, who turn away sharply when they catch him looking.

"I guess just Pinkie." Lily thinks of Pinkie, her sunken cheeks, her skin as dry and dead as Alfred's. Her body is coated in soft, downy fuzz, the kind your body grows when you starve it. Pinkie says it's called "lanugo," relishing the exotic term. She says the hair keeps her warm. Lily doesn't particularly like Pinkie, but she's drawn to her the way you're compelled to look at the victims of car wrecks spread out on the side of the road. Besides, Pinkie is the only one in school who will talk to her. Everyone else treats her like a freak, which is saying a lot when you take into account who gets shuttled off to Catalyst. "She starves herself."

"Control," Pinkie had explained once, regurgitating information from her therapist. "Anorexia is about control, not weight. Controlling the body when you cannot control anything else."

"She'll eat when she's hungry," Alfred says.

"But she is hungry. All the time. That's the problem. She won't let herself eat."

"Torpor," Alfred says. "A state of mental or physical activity, or the dormant state of a hibernating animal."

"Last I checked," Lily says, "people don't hibernate."

"Sure they do." Alfred squeezes her hand, then threads his fingers through hers, and she lets him.

When they circle in front of the pet store, Alfred suggests they go in and hold some of the puppies displayed in the window. Lily refuses. The dogs always make Lily sad, their desperate faces, their shit smeared across the bottoms of their cages for everyone to see. She knows from TV exposés that dead kittens and puppies wrapped in plastic bags are shoved in the freezers in the back room until disposing of them becomes convenient.

So they go to Applebee's instead, which is just opening but

already crowded with the early church crowd. Alfred requests that they sit in the smoking section, and the minute they settle in a booth, he pulls out a cigarette from the pack he keeps in his shirt pocket and lights it. With his sunglasses and fedora and cigarette, he kind of does resemble some aging star crashing and burning right there under the potted fern.

"Are you sure that's a good idea?" Lily says. People are staring at Alfred. His oxygen tank is propped at his feet like an obedient pet.

"Probably not." After each draw, he hacks uncontrollably, but it doesn't stop him from lighting another one off the butt of the first.

"My parents bring me here every Wednesday," Lily says. She reaches for the plate of nachos Alfred ordered but isn't touching, pushes a hunk of tortilla and cheese into her mouth. For the first time in months, she's starving. "They split last year, but my therapist thinks a pretend family dinner is good for my stability. The pretend dinners aren't much different than the ones we had before Dad left. How's school? Strange kind of weather we're having. That kind of crap. But the nachos are good."

Lily thinks of her parents, how they sit across from her, faking comfort in each other's presence, and watch every move she makes, as if she might slit her wrists at the table, bleed out on the Applebee's dessert menu. Her father moved out last year, right before Jessica died. Both of her parents like barbecues, cold beer, Neil Diamond, and bingo. Some stretch this into a marriage, and they did, and then they didn't.

Since then, her father lost ten pounds, started tanning,

found a new girlfriend he doesn't think Lily knows about. Her mother dyed her hair blond, started taking Jazzercise, buys books on how to release her inner French girl. They both look happier than Lily's ever seen them, and she hates them for it.

"My wife left me years ago," Alfred says. "Probably the best decision she ever made. I could have done better by her." He doesn't say how he did her wrong.

A middle-aged woman in a nice suit seated at the table next to theirs begins fanning her face in extravagant motions. Alfred reaches for another cigarette and lights it. He blows a river of smoke straight at the lady, then lifts his sunglasses to the top of his head and peers pointedly at the smoking section sign. The woman jumps at the sight of his mangled eye, studies her plate.

"I started smoking these in 'Nam," Alfred says, ashing his cigarette in the empty plate of nachos. "So in a way, that damn war killed me yet." He smiles. Lily smiles, too. She is beginning to enjoy how uncomfortable Alfred is making those around them, the increased shifting of bodies, the quick glances at their table, the uppity woman fanning her face.

"You were in a war?" Lily doesn't know much about the history of the Vietnam War, and what she does know comes from movies—*Platoon, Hamburger Hill, Full Metal Jacket.* She's immediately fascinated by Alfred's hands, the idea that they once held a gun or a grenade, that the hand she'd been holding earlier might have pulled the trigger that ended a life.

"Did you kill anybody?" she asks.

Alfred blinks rapidly, his bad eyelid out of sync with the good one, and immediately Lily knows she's asked the wrong question. A series of emotions flit across his face, the contortions of his mouth and eyes so exaggerated, he looks almost like a cartoon.

"My best friend was murdered," Lily says quickly—too quickly. "He dumped her in the woods. Like a bad afterschool special. Her mother pretty much lost it. She forgot to pick her up from cheerleading practice, and Jessica decided to walk." Lily feels sick to her stomach, as if she's used Jessica to make Alfred like her or forgive her or feel sorry for her, and she knows that somewhere Jessica is watching and has seen how easily Lily sold her out. And then she's pissed, because Jessica is the one who put her in this position to begin with, getting her in as much trouble in death as she did when alive. So she adds, "I hate her. I hate her for being so stupid."

She waits for Alfred to give her the look she gets when she talks about Jessica, which is almost never, the oh-poor-girl-you're-fucked-in-the-head-for-life look. But he just smokes thoughtfully for a minute, then says, "I blew off my buddy's left ass cheek when he went to take a leak. They call it friendly fire, but he didn't seem to think it was so friendly."

"Really." Lily giggles. "That would suck." She thinks of the idiot in *Full Metal Jacket,* the one who gets picked on all the time by the asshole drill sergeant. How the idiot can't take it anymore, so he blows the sergeant to bits before taking his own head off in the bathroom. How his blood splatters everywhere. She wonders if an ass cheek would explode the same way.

"Nah," Alfred says. "But you seemed sad. I thought that would cheer you up."

"I bet my mother would love someone to accidentally blow

off her fat thighs," Lily says. "She spends enough time working on them."

Alfred's face jerks and then is serious in that startling way his moods change, which is often. "It's a terrible thing, Queenie," he says, "being responsible for a life. Yours or anyone else's."

But Lily can't help wondering what it's like—that kind of power. And she wants to ask him how it feels to have death inside of you and to know it, to feel your lungs deflate and wither, to carry that in you like some freaky gestation, but he's waving down the waitress, asking for a Coors.

When the waitress leaves, Alfred reaches for yet another cigarette, lights it, coughs, then puts his head in both hands, the tip of the cigarette looming precariously close to the oxygen tubes dangling around his neck.

He stays like this for a minute, not moving, the ash from his cigarette sifting to the table. "Iniquity," he says finally, looking up at her. His face is white as a sheet. "A gross injustice or wickedness." Then, "I'm sorry, Queenie, but I don't feel so good."

• • •

Lily's not used to driving a stick, and each time she misses a gear, Alfred groans from the backseat, then laughs at his groan, then groans at his laugh. Lily has no idea where she is going. Alfred lives in a seedy part of town she never knew existed. He offers directions (left at the Conoco, right at the Laundromat, left at the rib joint), but he always seems to be about two blocks behind. It takes them half an hour to drive the five miles from the mall to Alfred's house.

When they get there, a white box with two windows and a door, Alfred slips out of the backseat and lurches up the front steps, his oxygen tank banging on each step so hard, Lily wonders if he secretly wants it to explode. The door is unlocked, and he stumbles in, then throws himself on the couch.

Lily stands in the doorway, unsure of what to do. The house is barren. A couch, a milk crate, a radio. Nothing else. Not one book or magazine or photo or painting.

"Shut the door," Alfred says, his hand over his face. "You're letting the cool air out."

As far as Lily can tell, there is no air-conditioning, but she steps inside and shuts the door, not moving any farther into the living room. She runs her tongue over her lip piercings, a nervous tic. When Alfred points wordlessly at the milk crate next to the couch, she shakes her head no, and he keeps pointing until she dutifully walks toward him and settles onto the crate.

"Nice place you got here," Lily says. She's trying to recapture the mood they had at Applebee's and the community center, because this is new territory for her, being in the home of a strange adult without her parents, an adult who doesn't seem to find anything peculiar about hanging out with a teenage girl, talking to her about wars and lovers and lost lives.

Alfred leans up on both elbows, the mangled eye and the tubes racing up his nostrils making him look like some science experiment gone wrong. "Anybody ever tell you not to go home with strangers?" he says. He falls back onto the couch. "Didn't your mama teach you anything?"

Lily's heart is in her belly, pounding low and hard, all her senses sharp. She can smell him, the warm wood scent. She can taste the stale air of a sickroom, hear water dripping somewhere, dogs barking in the distance. She wonders if this was what Jessica felt like—that afternoon she climbed into a stranger's car and knew things might not go her way—as if she were truly aware of being alive for the first time.

"Where's all your stuff?" Lily asks.

"Penitence," Alfred says. "Regret for wrongdoing. I gave it away to the neighbors." He laughs. "Some of these people have never had air-conditioning in their entire lives. When I gave them my window units, they cranked them. After they got the first electric bill, they traded them for booze or TVs. I swear those units have swapped hands a dozen times by now."

"You could've at least kept some pictures or something. I'd kill myself staring at a blank wall all day."

Alfred shrugs. "I don't want anything that makes me remember."

They sit this way for a while, the slow whirl of the ceiling fan doing nothing more than stirring up dust. Alfred's shirt is drenched in sweat, and Lily can see the pink of his skin under the cheap cotton fabric. His chest is thin, and Lily thinks of the women who have lain against it, what they said to him, what they promised.

She thinks he has fallen asleep when he opens his eyes and pats the side of the couch. "Come a bit closer," he says. "I want to see you."

Lily scoots the crate toward him until her legs are pressed against the couch, and he takes her hand and folds it into his.

"You're right lovely, Queenie," Alfred says, dragging his thumb across the soft skin on the inside of her wrist. "You shouldn't hide it. Someone will take it from you for good sooner or later. Then you'll spend the rest of the time you got trying to remember you when you were you."

"Maybe," Lily says. With her free hand, she reaches for his face, touches the puckered scar at the edge of his eye. It is shockingly hot.

"You never asked me about my eye," Alfred says. "I don't think anyone's spent more than an hour with me without asking about my eye."

"You never asked me what I want to do after high school," Lily says. "Or if I have a boyfriend. Or if I have nightmares. Or if I want to talk about it. Or"—she smiles—"my real name."

When he tugs on Lily's hands, she slips to her knees, and he drapes her across his emaciated chest, which Lily knows must pain him, any weight on those frail lungs, as delicate now as moth wings. His chin feels like sandpaper on her forehead.

"I'm not going to hurt you," he says. She can feel his small tremors as he breathes.

"I know," Lily says, and for the first time in a long time, she believes what she is saying.

ava bean

On the way home from the hospital, Ava tells Charlotte that after her first husband was killed during a German air attack on Bari in 1943, she cried without pause for weeks, only to emerge from her stunning grief temporarily blind. She blames this temporary disability for the early demise of her screen career.

"No one wants a *real* blind person in a film," Ava says from the backseat of the Chevette. Charlotte watches in the rearview mirror as the old woman rummages through a Burger King bag propped on the cast that covers her leg from toe to hip. She throws handfuls of salt and ketchup on the floorboard, finally finds the French fries, shoves a handful in her mouth.

"Fake blind, sure," Ava says with her mouth full. "But when you're bopping off the set and knocking things over, well, let's just say you draw the wrong kind of attention to yourself."

"You'd think it'd make you look more authentic,"

Charlotte says, pulling into the narrow gravel strip that runs between Ava's house and the neighbor's to the right.

"Nobody wants authentic," Ava says. "We're all so brainwashed that fake usually seems realer than real. Like if your kids never call or visit or send Christmas cards, and you go about your business, feeding the dog and making dinner, because you have to, because no one else is going to do it for you—those same kids might think that you don't care, that you ain't dying inside." Ava points a limp French fry at her chest, mimicking a dagger slipping into her heart. "Now if an actor in that situation on TV cried and threw things and called the children in the middle of the night begging for attention, something no one who thinks anything of herself would actually do, the people watching would say, 'That's real.' "

On the sidewalk, a toddler stumbles in circles. Braids poke out of the Tupperware bowl she wears on her head. Occasionally the girl whacks the bowl with a carrot she carries like a wand, and Charlotte thinks of Lucy, her long pigtails, the way they glowed in the fading sunlight one afternoon at the beach, a long-ago memory that has fused into all the others.

Ava's neighbor, the toddler's great-grandmother, is sprawled across a fold-out chair on her front lawn, her thick legs mottled by the sun. She shakes a fly swatter at Charlotte's Chevette, yells something in an indistinguishable European language.

"The neighborhood is going to hell in a handbasket," Ava says, rolling down her window. "I thought that was the whole point of the war, to take care of these heathens." Then, to the neighbor, "I've told you, this is my goddamn driveway."

"I can park on the street," Charlotte offers.

"I got my sight back in an A&P," Ava is saying as she struggles to reach over her cast-encased leg to open the back door. "That's the God's truth. I was groping along the produce bins when *boom.* I must've passed out, 'cause when I came to, I could see as clear as I'm seeing you, clearer even since now I can't seem to see a damn thing, and there was a sign hanging over me, 'Jonathan apples, ten cents a pound,' which wasn't a bad price. Produce is outrageous these days."

"Hold on," Charlotte says, getting out of the car. When Charlotte opens the back door, Ava begins scooting off the seat, her cast missiled straight toward Charlotte's belly. By the time Ava is propped against the dented Chevette with her crutches under her arms, Charlotte's new shirt is covered in the old woman's makeup. Ava had refused to leave the hospital until Charlotte helped apply her "face," the pasty, exaggerated mask Ava has worn every day of her adult life.

The neighbor yells something garbled, something that sounds like "whore."

"The food." Ava points into the car. Charlotte crawls into the backseat, grabs the Burger King, pops the greasy bag under one arm, Ava under the other, and they stumble-hop toward the house.

"He didn't mean to do it, you know," Ava says at the front door while Charlotte fumbles for the keys. "Ralph's a good dog. Not a mean bone in his body. He'd never hurt me on purpose."

"I know," Charlotte says. Ralph lets loose a wretched, hollow wail from the foyer. For a moment, Charlotte regrets that she didn't take Billy's advice and dump the dog in the woods when Ava was in the hospital and she'd had the chance.

"You're a good girl, too," Ava says.

• • •

"How long you been living here?" Billy asks.

"Four weeks," Charlotte says. She's sitting on the front porch, sipping a beer and smoking, watching Billy rake the leaves. Ava passed out after her fifth glass of wine, and Charlotte put her to bed. The sun is barely sinking, but Ava won't wake up until morning. Charlotte considers herself off duty, although the agreement is she's on call 24/7.

"I'm just saying." Billy pokes the pile of leaves with the rake. "I've been working around here for near ten years, and you don't see her offering *me* any sweet deal. You know what she calls me? She calls me boy. Me—almost fifty. Might as well say nigger. Means the same thing."

"She's old. Old people around here are set in their ways." Charlotte thinks Billy might be good-looking if he weren't so skinny, if he weren't so angry.

Billy stops raking, stares at Charlotte. His irises are almost as black as his pupils, and Charlotte finds it difficult to return his gaze.

"Old," Billy says, then snorts. "Are you an idiot girl? You think that woman just has herself a light, even tan? That she won't leave the house without all that makeup because she's out to catch herself a man? You ever see her kids around here? Any of them? She's got three, and the oldest owns this house. Now why do you think he'd buy his mama a house in Florida when he lives halfway across the world in California? Not one of them kids ever visits. And you know why?" He pokes his arm out, points with one gloved finger at his dun-colored skin. "That's why. Her kids didn't come out light like her. They can't pass. You see what I'm saying?"

Charlotte isn't sure what Billy's saying, because Billy says a lot. For instance, he says that Zelda, the next-door neighbor, was married to a Nazi, and she's hiding out here in Twilight Pines to keep a low profile. He says that the butcher down at the Piggly Wiggly woos boys into the freezer with Hershey bars and toy gadgets he steals from cereal boxes, that he's seen this with his own eyes. He says that Clinton is a Russian spy who's bent on ruining the country, which might not be such a bad thing, considering that the country has been going straight downhill since they elected the android actor from California.

"She's always been nice to me," Charlotte says, which is not exactly the case. She crushes her cigarette against the concrete porch and adds it to the pile beside the potted plant. "I was living in my car when she found me."

Charlotte wasn't so much living in her car as passed out in it with nowhere in particular to go and all her things crammed in plastic crates in her trunk. She was considering going back home to Montgomery, where things were fucked up, but at least in a way she understood. She'd stopped for a drink or two at the bar on the corner and woke up in her car in front of Ava's house, Ava rapping on her window. The old woman took Charlotte inside, fed her, let her wash up, and after Charlotte repaid the kindness by listening to some of Ava's life stories, which included the one where the handsome heart specialist with the diamond pinky ring and the uppity secretary told Ava she was going to die sooner rather than later, Ava offered Charlotte a job as a caretaker of sorts. She gets room and board, a weekly allowance, and when Ava dies, a tidy bonus. Charlotte never considered saying no.

"Mrs. Bean thinks you're weak, that she can own you, that she's on her way out and you're her Hail Mary, her last chance to convince someone she ain't the mean-hearted bitch she is," Billy says. "You being white makes it all the better." He cups his hands together, peers into the little cave he's made, like there's a trapped animal in there.

Charlotte gestures at the crumbling Cape Cod behind her. "Things worked out good. She's got someone to take care of her, I got a place to stay."

"I'm just saying. Mrs. Bean seemed to be doing just fine until you came around, and then *bam,* that little mutt pulls her down the stairs. Mighty convenient for you, don't you think? You almost hit the big payday." He walks toward Charlotte, rips a glove off with his teeth, covers her knee with his bare hand, the rough pad of his thumb moving in tiny circles. This is the first time a man has touched her in a year. "Maybe," he says, "you're smarter than she thought."

● ● ●

"Marlene Dietrich was a man-hungry bitch," Ava says. "I had a good role in *Destry Rides Again.* Three lines. Long ones at that. But she was getting old by then, and she didn't like the competition. They cut me. Not one 'I'm sorry.' "

Ava holds Ralph to her chest with one speckled hand, a cigarette dangles from the other. Charlotte is setting Ava's long, thinning hair, and it's difficult to get the uneven strands to stay wrapped around the rollers. Every time Charlotte's fingers come near Ralph, he gives her a little nip, which makes Ava, who is past drunk, giggle. In front of them, over the kitchen table, hangs a full-length painting of a pale naked woman with three perfect breasts. Her nipples are accented with tinted glass shards. Ava says that it's high art, that it's Charlotte's after she dies, that she'll make sure of it.

"I've got a daughter, you know," Ava says as she fumbles ashes into a giant Chinese vase, which Charlotte knows holds the remains of Ava's third husband, a man she refers to only as The Bastard.

Ava's hair feels silky against Charlotte's hands, not like the wiry hair she expects on a black woman, and she thinks of the soft lock of hair she keeps in a Bible in her bedroom, the way it feels when she fans it against the sensitive skin of her eyelids.

"So I'm content it turned out that way," Ava is saying. "If Tina had to be one or the other, I'm glad it was smart rather than pretty. I was pretty, and it got me nothing but heartache. She was smart, and it got her a doctor from Malibu who can make her look like whatever she damn well pleases. If we'd had the same options when I was working Hollywood, there's no telling how far I could have gone." She dumps her cigarette butt into the vase, then peers down into its opening. "Looks like The Bastard is filling up. He always was full of himself."

"I think you still look beautiful," Charlotte says. "How many women your age have hair like this?" She pats Ava's hair, which in spite of being freshly washed already reeks of cigarette smoke.

"It's funny, being blind," Ava says. "Your senses get really sharp. I could tell what kind of fruit was in a bowl without touching it, only smelling. I could hear someone enter the room just by the breathing." She pauses, scratches Ralph behind his ears. "And I can still smell bullshit from a mile away."

Charlotte's hands stop mid-roll. Sometimes, not often, Ava gets mean when she drinks. Throws things when Charlotte tells her it's time to eat or go to bed. Shits herself out of spite. When she does these things, Charlotte almost wishes that when Ralph pulled Ava down the stairs, the fall had killed the woman instead of just breaking her leg, wishes she could take the money now and go somewhere new, start over right this time.

Ava leans back in her chair, tilts her face toward Charlotte, stares at her for a long moment, her gray eyes shadowy. "You ain't pretty, neither," she says finally, "but at least you try to be nice to a dying old lady. Nice is better than pretty any day of the week. That's what I told Tina when she was little, but it just made her meaner. She's never visited me here in Florida. Won't even take my calls these days. Can you imagine, knowing your mama's got maybe six months and not taking her calls? What kind of hate is that? The kind that kills you the long, hard way, that's what kind." She kicks the vase with her good foot, and old Ralph releases an irritated bleat. "Just ask The Bastard."

Charlotte understands the complexities of families, and she tells Ava so. Then she begins sharing the story of her father, how he couldn't keep his job. How he woke her mother up from a dead sleep when he came in after the bar closed, knowing she worked two full-time jobs, and forced her to make him breakfast, eggs and bacon, the whole works. How he kept a lover, a tiny Vietnamese woman who did laundry, for ten years and two babies, not that he took care of them, either. How he came to her mother's funeral drunk and had to be dragged out of the cemetery by her uncle. How his hate didn't kill him before he held up a convenience store and shot a widow straight through the eye for less than eighty bucks. How when Charlotte went to visit him that one time in prison to make things right after Lucy was born, after she understood what it meant to be a parent, to bring a child into the world, he refused to come to the visitation room, said he didn't know anyone by the name of Charlotte.

But Ava is snoring before she can finish, her hair only half-rolled, the rest already drying in a long frizz.

"She out?"

Charlotte turns to see Billy standing in the doorway, twilight glowing behind him so that he's haloed in russet gold, and for a moment, Charlotte cannot speak. She simply nods.

Billy stomps through the kitchen, his dirty boots leaving tracks on the floor. He stops, stares at Ava. "I ain't ever touched her before," he says. "Not even to take my pay. She just leaves it on the back porch in an envelope."

"Why do you think she hired you and kept you around all this time if she can't stand to look at you? Why would she punish herself like that?" Charlotte grabs Ava's half-finished bottle of wine from the table, takes a long drink, trying the whole time not to look at Billy, who's staring at her as though he might want to hit her.

"Who knows," he says finally, "why we all hate ourselves so much."

Billy pulls off his baseball cap and sets it on the table with the solemn air of a boy in church, then he plucks up Ava from her chair, her cast swinging, and walks to the back of the house toward the master bedroom. Charlotte follows closely behind, Ralph yipping at her feet. When Billy stops in the doorway of Ava's bedroom, Charlotte almost runs into his narrow back.

"I ain't ever been in this room. Not to fix a broken window or a squeaky board or nothing. She always uses a company if something goes wrong in here."

"Like I told you," Charlotte says, "old people are stuck in their ways."

Billy turns toward her sharply. "Can you not say something stupid for five minutes, just long enough to get her in the bed?"

He walks through the doorway, and Charlotte runs to the bed and yanks down the white crocheted comforter, not bothering to pull down the sheets. Billy lowers Ava onto the bed with surprising gentleness, arranges her hands to cover her sagging bosom. Charlotte grabs two pillows from the trunk at the end of the bed to slide under Ava's injured leg, hugs them protectively in front of her.

Ava's eyes flutter open, lock on Billy. "What the hell is he doing here?" she says, quite clearly considering, and then she's asleep again.

"Nice law-abiding old lady, right?" Billy thumbs through a stack of envelopes on Ava's bedside table. "How do you reckon she gets five different Social Security checks? You ever thought about that? About where your money's coming from?"

"It's the same money that pays you," Charlotte says, and immediately she regrets it. Billy frowns, slams the envelopes down on the table. Ralph, who is half-blind, barks at the commotion, then bites at Billy's boot. Billy kicks him hard in the ribs, says, "That goddamn dog has bit me for the last time." Ralph growls, teeters around dazed for a second, then flops down next to the bed.

"You know how easy it would be?" Billy says, nodding toward the pillows Charlotte is still clamping against her chest. "A minute at most, and it would all be over. Then you'd have your money." Charlotte shoves the pillows under Ava's leg before he can say anything else. He walks up behind her, cups his hands over her breasts, places his lips against her hair. "I'm just teasing you, girl," he says. "I like teasing you." Then, "Was that true, what you said about your daddy?" He doesn't move his hands.

"True enough," Charlotte says.

"Let's go somewhere else," he whispers against her neck. "I never feel right in this house."

• • •

The neighbor, Zelda, has parked her rusting Lincoln behind Charlotte's Chevette, which happens often in the ongoing driveway wars.

Billy works a brick loose from one of the planters lining Ava's porch, shrugs off his T-shirt, wraps it around his hand, then slams the brick through the Lincoln's driver's-side window. He pokes his hand carefully through the broken glass, unlocks the door, opens it, then leans into the car, puts it into neutral, and starts pushing it off the gravel strip that runs between their houses and onto Zelda's lawn. The wiry muscles on his dark back shimmy under his skin.

"There," he says after the Lincoln is soundly on Zelda's front lawn. "Fucking Nazi bitch."

Charlotte thinks that she shouldn't go off with this man, that perhaps he is indeed as dangerous as he seems. But she can still feel his breath against her neck, his hands cupping her breasts, and it's been a year. She's been real good for a year.

"I'll drive," he says. He shakes the glass out of his shirt, then tugs it back over his head. When he's dressed, he grins at her, says, "Got to look good for our date."

"This is a date?" Charlotte says.

"Gimme the keys." He shoves his hand toward her, palm out. "I got a place I go."

They drive out of Twilight Pines, past Check into Cash, past the Piggly Wiggly, past the Keep It Clean Laundromat, and pull into Charley's Fine Liquors, where a group of young black men, their pants dangling low, mill about slouch-backed in the parking lot.

"Nervous?" Billy says. He places a finger under a lock of Charlotte's fair hair, flicks it. "You think they'd hurt you if they could?"

"Grey Goose," Charlotte says. "And make sure it's cold." She hands him two twenties. This is the first time she's had any kind of money in months.

Charlotte watches him enter the store, the way he nods gamely at the young men, slapping a few on the back as he passes. Billy says something to one boy, a squat kid with a goatee. The boy looks toward the Chevette and starts laughing. Charlotte slams the lock down on her door, then unlocks it just as quickly, not wanting to give Billy any ammunition to work with.

When Billy gets back to the car, he shoves a bottle of cheap wine toward her, tucks two 40's between his thighs.

They drive out of town, toward the suburbs where all the stucco houses come in shades of pink, nice, clean-looking houses with a few palm trees growing here and there on tidy, manicured lawns. Billy has rolled down the windows. The rush of air when the car's moving fast makes it possible to talk only at stoplights, not that they do.

"Here we go," Billy says finally, turning slowly into a fancy circle of houses that faces a man-made lake strategically lit with dim spotlights. A fake heron perches on the bank. "I used to work out here when they were building this place. The pond is stocked right. I fished in it some mornings before work until some rich fucker complained that he didn't pay dues for any Tom, Dick, or Harry to steal his bass. They usually don't bother you if you just want to stare at the water."

He takes the bottle of wine from Charlotte, screws off the cap, then hands it back to her. "Cheers."

Billy signals that he doesn't want to talk by turning the radio on low, some light jazz station Charlotte never listens to. They drink quietly for a while. The wine, mixed with the pain pills Charlotte's been swiping from Ava, hits harder than she expects, and her head's spinning before half the bottle is gone.

"You ready?" Billy asks. Charlotte nods. He takes her wine and wedges their bottles behind the backseat, then leans toward her, begins unbuttoning her blouse, his fingers icy from the beer.

Charlotte closes her eyes. She's sixteen and lying in a field with Lucy's father, right in the middle of the day. They are naked, their bodies damp from lovemaking. They wave wildly at cars driving by on the county road. Some of the cars honk as they pass, and it feels as though everyone is part of their love story.

"You smell good, girl," Billy's saying, and then his lips are hot against her breastbone, his breath musky and sweet. Charlotte thinks, It's been so long. She thinks, This feels so good. And his lips are moving, down, down her chest, against the rim of her bra, and her head is spinning. She feels weightless, like air.

When she opens her eyes again, Billy's leaning against the driver's door, smoking.

"What happened?" she asks. Her shirt is completely unbuttoned. Her skirt is pushed up to her waist. There is a new, fist-size dent on the glove compartment door.

"Sorry about the car," Billy says, looking at the dent. "You passed out on me."

Charlotte reaches between her thighs, feels for moisture.

"I'm many things," Billy says, "but a rapist ain't one of them." He thumps his cigarette out the window.

"Why are you always so angry?" Charlotte says without knowing she's going to say it. For a second, the time it takes to draw a single breath, his face twitches and softens, and Charlotte can see there's a way in, a way for her to touch all that hurt and want moiling there in the pit of him. And then he's Billy again. This is her weakness. Charlotte knows. This is the kind of man, all of that barely restrained anger, that makes her feel alive. She didn't need the fat-assed condescending social worker to tell her that. She's always known.

"Can you take a break from asking stupid questions?" Billy

snaps. "You must be worn out thinking them all up by now." He presses a hand hard against the C-section scar on her belly. "Where's the kid?"

Charlotte pushes his hand away, pulls her shirt over her chest. "They took her."

Charlotte sees Lucy's face in the rear window of the cruiser, her sweet, sad face. The cops didn't even bother to buckle the girl in, and they'd said she was the one guilty of child endangerment. Charlotte sees herself mouthing, "I'll get you soon, baby," at the disappearing cruiser, but even then, in that exact moment she mouthed the words, she knew she wouldn't. That in a way, it would be so much easier not to.

"Where's the father?" Billy says. "He still around?" His voice drops when he says this, and Charlotte thinks that maybe he is jealous. Just a little bit.

"It's been a long time," she says.

"I got a kid." He points at one of the more modest houses surrounded by a moat of light. "He lives there. He asked me not to come around anymore. But sometimes I come here and watch. He's done good for himself, you know? That means I've done good. That's how I like to think about it, anyway."

"You've done better than most," Charlotte says.

"How much is Mrs. Bean paying you?"

Charlotte considers not telling him but figures he probably already knows. He has a way of knowing everything. "A hundred and fifty a week, ten thousand when she passes. The doctor said she's got six months, tops. With the added trauma of the leg, maybe not that long."

"You get it in writing?" He pulls a cigarette from his pack, places it between her lips, curves his hand around the match while he lights it for her.

She nods yes, blows out a stream of smoke. "Not getting things in writing is how I ended up sleeping in my car in the first place."

"It's funny, death," he says. "Even when we know it's coming, it's never expected, not really. Like that boy in the papers on death row in Texas. I mean, he was wormy in the head, but even an animal knows when it's on its way out, and I'm betting he was smarter than most animals. They give him his last meal, and he doesn't finish it. Tells them to wrap it up. That he'll finish it when he gets back. You see what I'm saying?"

"Was Ava really in the movies?" Charlotte asks. "Do you think she has the kind of money she promised me?" She has spent weeks staring at the black-and-white framed photos scattered around Ava's house, women in shiny dresses cut on the bias, costume jewelry dripping from necks and ears. Charlotte can't tell if they're actual photos or reproductions bought from some souvenir store. She likes to imagine Ava as young and glamorous, drinking cocktails in long white gloves at Hollywood mansions in the hills, not old and drunk and dying. She wants to believe that this kind of glamour happens for someone. And she wants to believe that Ava will really give her the money she offered, that the agreement she requested Ava to write out and sign is worth more than the paper it's written on.

Billy snorts. "Stupid, sweet girl," he says. "If that woman's got money, you ain't getting it unless you take it." He cradles her chin, leans toward her as though he's going to kiss her. "It would be so easy," he says. "A few too many pills. An honest mistake.

It could take years for her to be dead and done with it. Doctors never get it right. How about Mexico? We could rent ourselves a little hacienda." He laughs at the exotic word. Repeats it. "Hacienda."

His other hand is kneading her belly now, and her blood is warming, her heart quickening.

Then his finger is inside her, pushing hard, the way she likes it. "You want to try again?" he says.

• • •

When Charlotte knocks on the neighbor's door, Zelda opens it in midrant, the foreign words tumbling out of her mouth, hard as pebbles. She clutches an official-looking document in one hand, and she won't shut up, no matter how politely Charlotte smiles.

"This is America," Charlotte finally interrupts, "I speak English."

"Deed," Zelda says, pointing at the document she's now waving in Charlotte's face. "Do you understand this word? My driveway."

"I'm just looking for Mrs. Bean's dog," Charlotte says. "He's gone missing."

"This is no Germany," Zelda says. The freckled pouches under her eyes quiver, and Charlotte realizes that the woman is on the verge of tears. "You cannot take my things."

"I'm just looking for the dog, ma'am," Charlotte says.

"Maybe the criminals that place my car on my yard took it." Zelda smiles. "Maybe they do many bad things around here." Then she slams the door in Charlotte's face.

When Charlotte gets home, she finds Ava sitting at the kitchen table with an empty bottle of wine, her crutches tossed at her feet. A thin line of blood seeps down her forehead, but she doesn't move to wipe it away.

"I fell," she says.

Charlotte walks to the kitchen sink, opens the cupboard, pulls out the large basin she uses to wash Ava's hair, and begins filling it with water. She grabs the shampoo from on top of the refrigerator and sets it on the table.

"It's been a week," Ava says. She's crying now. Makeup clots under her eyes. Her lipstick is smeared across her cheek. "Ralph never leaves my sight. Where could he have gone?"

"We'll find him," Charlotte says, slipping a dishtowel around Ava's neck. "He can't have gone far. Somebody found him, and they're just holding him safe until we get him. You'll see." She knows this is not true. Either Ralph crawled off to die or Billy dumped him in the countryside or Zelda finally found a way to get back at Ava and the rest of the world for the many injustices she's suffered; but wherever Ralph is, he isn't coming back. For now, the lie seems kinder.

Charlotte massages Ava's knotted hands until the basin fills. She lugs it to the kitchen table, scoots Ava's stool around until her lower back is pressed against the edge of the basin, then lowers the woman's head into the water. Her hair is matted with blood, and Charlotte is relieved when she sees that the cut looks worse than it is.

"He's the only one that loves me," Ava is saying as Charlotte soaps her hair, so thin that the scalp shows through. Pink-tinged suds cover Charlotte's hands. "My kids don't give a damn.

Not a one of them. Only him. He didn't mean to hurt me. He doesn't have a mean bone in his body."

"I know," Charlotte says. She dips Ava's head into the basin, tries to get out as much shampoo and blood as she can.

Ava jerks up. "What did you do with him?" Water splashes on the tile floor, a mess Charlotte will have to clean. Ava grips Charlotte's hand, the long nails breaking the skin. "Where did you put him?"

"Shhhh," Charlotte whispers, and Ava relaxes, rests her head back against the basin.

"There was a woman in the hospital bed next to me, when I broke my leg," Ava says sleepily. "She'd been in some kind of accident. Her and her husband. Not a scratch on her, but she'd hit her head and couldn't remember nothing you just told her. Her husband was killed, and her kids would tell her and she'd go crazy, and then she'd take a nap, wake up all confused, but happy, you know—happy to be here, but clueless that her husband was gone. And then they'd have to tell her all over that her old man had died, and she'd lose it again." Ava stares up at Charlotte, heavy-lidded, her eyes unfocused. "What do you think is worse—forgetting or knowing?"

Charlotte is trying not to listen to Ava. She's trying to remember Lucy's father, what he said to her when he touched her, how young they were, how they believed the things they told each other. She's trying to remember Lucy as a baby when she used to bathe her in a basin like this, her chubby baby legs kicking against the water. If Charlotte closes her eyes, she can feel Lucy's fingers curl around her thumb, she can hear her shriek with laughter.

Until Lucy, Charlotte didn't understand anything about how the world works, about how one person can shape the course of another's life as much by absence as anything else, how a stranger's trust might be the closest thing to salvation you're ever offered.

Ava is asleep now, the full weight of her head pressing against Charlotte's hands. She holds her there, suspended over the water. For one forgiving moment, the weight is not unbearable.

blue moon

On lazy days, me and Misty sat on the back porch and waited to see if the funeral home boys would load up the hearse for a ceremony. There were only two cemeteries in town, and both a few blocks away, but people around those parts still liked a jazzy show, so old Mr. Garret, the owner/director/mortician, would put on his dark suit and his derby hat, shine up the seventies Cadillac hearse, and take the body for a spin down Main Street—past the Capitol building and Gilda's Touch of Class Salon and the Feed and Seed—before heading to the unofficially white cemetery or the unofficially black cemetery, depending on who'd died, of course.

Misty inherited the Victorian we lived in from an old aunt the year before. Living that close to a funeral home had made Misty philosophical about life in general, and she'd often ask me, "Eva, if you could have one thing in this world, what would it be?"

I'd say, "A thing called love," or, "A mansion over

the hilltop" or, "Less conversation and a little more action," and Misty would look sad like usual, bury her head in her giant hands, and say, "Can't anybody around here take things serious?"

I'd moved in with Misty, who'd been my best friend since before we could walk, after my husband left me because I'd spent the last of our savings on a polyester, flared-leg jumpsuit with semiprecious gemstones lining the collar. He moved in with his mother out on Highway 49. Where the lights stay on all year, he'd said. Where there were other kinds of food besides ramen noodles. Where we didn't have to water down the cereal milk to make it last the week. Things were bad, but it wasn't really about the money.

"Henry," I'd said as he was packing his things. I gave him my mournful stare—the look he'd loved when we still wanted each other bad enough to lie about who we really were. "We can't go on together with suspicious minds."

"You know what you need?" my mother-in-law told me when I called to let her know Henry was on his way. "You need to go out and get your hair done. Maybe your nails, too. White tipped like those French. Make yourself feel special. Think of it like a little vacation."

She'd been wanting her boy back ever since we got hitched in Vegas a few years before, and after talking to her, whatever hope I had that she'd send him home to me flew right out the window.

Hope, I'd decided, was possibly a terminal ailment.

I said just this to Misty on the afternoon we watched two boys heft Pearl Stringer's casket into the back of Mr. Garret's hearse.

Pearl had been trying to convince her husband, Hubert, to get off the couch and find a job for years. Finally, he had enough of it and put a gun in his mouth and took care of business with a focus that might have made Pearl proud under different circumstances. Unfortunately, the bullet cut a path through him and found its way to Pearl's heart, which Hubert never could do, and she dropped dead on one of the rag rugs she made and sold at the local A&P. Hubert died two days later and would be buried beside Pearl in a separate ceremony tomorrow.

"I think it's kind of romantic," Misty said. "Even though things were bad between them, the bond of marriage was stronger. Of course they would die by a single bullet."

"Bond of marriage," I coughed. "You say that because you ain't ever been married."

Misty tugged on the fat bellies of her cheeks, which meant I'd hurt her feelings. This was before she married Daniel the Bible thumper, and she was a twenty-four-year-old virgin and felt tragic for it. Misty was a big girl. And I mean big. She tried to hide it by wearing black gothic dresses—summer and winter—that looked like she'd stolen somebody's curtains.

Misty could have dated a lot. She had that firm kind of roundness some men love. But she'd convinced herself that any man who hit on her was the kind of man who settled for a fat girl, and like all of us, Misty wanted more.

So, instead, she scoured the papers for any kind of love story that seemed fate driven and inevitable and turned any tale between a couple—like Henry leaving or Pearl getting shot—into something more than it was, which was life kicking you in the ass for trying.

Her favorite was a story about a woman and man who'd had

a knock-down, drag-out a few towns over. After mauling each other for hours, the woman doused herself with gasoline and threatened to set herself on fire if her husband didn't get the hell out of her house. Apparently, this was the kind of passion he was looking for, and they made up and made love and decided things were good enough between them. Then she lit a cigarette, and you can pretty much picture how it ended. They patched her up as best they could over at UAB, and afterward he rolled her around in a wheelchair, telling everybody, "ain't she got the prettiest blue eyes," which was about all that was left of her.

"His love set her on fire," Misty liked to say, and when she said things like this, I thought maybe it was best that she didn't date.

"You'll find somebody," I said. I pointed to Mr. Garret's hearse, which was pulling out of the funeral home parking lot to take Pearl Stringer on her last tour of the town. "Let's just hope it doesn't end up like that."

"Well, somebody's got to love you a lot to care enough to kill you," Misty said. "That's all I'm saying."

"But he didn't mean to kill her," I said, and Misty scowled.

One of the funeral home boys, a black kid Mr. Garret called in from biking the streets and paid twenty bucks to lift things, like caskets, walked over, his red Coca-Cola T-shirt soaked in sweat.

"It sure is hot," he said, eyeing the six-pack I had cooling in a mop bucket at my feet.

"It's hotter in hell," Misty said. "That's where boys too young to drink end up."

The boy grinned, his smile big for his face. Most people in town thought Misty had gone half-crazy since moving into her aunt's house, and they egged her on by asking all sorts of questions about the meaning of the world, or offering little tidbits for her to chew on and distort into something revealing about life.

"Did you know they sew their assholes up?" he said slyly. "Mr. Garret let me watch. So the goop they put in them after they scoop everything clean don't leak out."

Misty looked horrified.

I laughed, tossed the boy a beer. "I bet Hubert Stringer wishes they'd sewn her mouth shut instead. According to Misty here, he'll be listening to it for eternity."

"Oh, they do that, too," the boy said, holding the cold beer against his forehead.

"Don't you have a show to get ready for?" Misty said to me, kicking my mop bucket. "That's all you need—to be drunk while performing community service for being drunk."

"I'm consistent, which is a kind of dependability," I said, taking a sip of the beer I had sandwiched between my thighs. It was the temperature of spit.

The boy drank the beer in one long swallow, then tossed the can in the pile I'd been working on next to the porch. He saluted me like a general, said, "Long live The King."

• • •

The Home for New Dreams was located in an old Baptist church that had been renovated into little apartments with shared kitchens and bathing facilities. About a dozen people lived there, including the manager and the nurse. Every year, one of the neighbors would go in front of the city council trying to get the home shut down, saying they were concerned about the tenants, who were all suffering from some kind of mental condition, setting the place on fire or molesting their kids or breaking into their homes. The tenants never caused many problems—an occasional streaking down Main Street (which plenty of normal folks had done), a scene on the lawn now and again when one didn't want to do what they were supposed to be doing. But some of them looked different, their faces a bit skewed or off balance, and some of them sang all the time, whether it was appropriate or not, and most of them stared at you unabashedly if they found you interesting, like children who didn't know any better, and this made the neighbors uneasy. No one likes a reminder of how vulnerable we all are.

When Henry'd left, I went on a bender that ended with me wrapping my Nova around a live oak in Mr. Nelson's backyard. It wasn't my best moment.

After telling the judge about Henry, how we'd been high school sweethearts and how I'd tried so hard to make it work and how I cooked meals for him and cleaned and tried to be a good wife, which he never appreciated because he resented my wanting to be a career woman, too, the judge went easy, giving me community service, which included performing for the Home for New Dreams.

I was in my new Elvis jumpsuit, and I squatted on my haunches so as not to get the white polyester dirty, pulled a cigarette from my purse and lit it, careful not to torch my glued-on sideburns, squirrel size. Some teenagers drove by in a beat-up convertible, summer skin bared, yelled, "Viva Las Vegas!"

I swung my cape over my shoulders and gave them the finger. They went wild.

"You come in?" a voice said, and I turned to see a tiny Asian woman with a moon face. "You here to sing?"

I thought of saying, No, lady, I'm just hanging out in Elvis gear, but then I thought maybe she didn't know who Elvis was, even though I thought I'd read somewhere that he was more popular than Jesus around the world.

They'd placed a ring of fold-up chairs around a little stage, and an older woman with yellow hair the color of underripe bananas was trying to get everyone seated. It looked like a scene from *One Flew over the Cuckoo's Nest.*

A teenager in a frilly pink dress more suited for a young girl was standing in one of the chairs, singing at the top of her lungs, "Blackbird singing in the dead of night, take these broken wings and learn to fly." She had a roll of toilet paper in her hands, and she'd roll it out, singing all the while, then roll it back up. She looked real happy with herself, and it struck me that maybe she had the right idea, maybe we'd all be better off not thinking so much.

"That's Sandy," the yellow-haired woman said to me. "She really likes her some Beatles. I hear that song when I sleep now, so it'll be nice to hear something new from you."

I'd been an impersonator for a few years by then, ever since Henry and I saw a show in Vegas on our honeymoon. I did Liza, Barbra, Madonna, but strangely enough, Elvis was my moneymaker and my passion. Henry'd loved it at first—the tight leather pants, a guitar slung over my shoulder, my hair dyed black and slanting into my eyes—until the gigs kept me out of town or made me miss dinner, and then he told me that with a voice like mine, I'd make a great secretary. That's when things started going downhill.

"You got a favorite?" I said.

"Anything but Beatles." She shook my hand. "I'm Margie." She gestured to the woman who'd let me in. "That's the nurse. Kim."

"You sing 'Lonesome Tonight'?" Kim said shyly.

A doughy man in a Superman shirt flew at me, his hands cradling his heart. "I have a soul," he said, the way a kid might say, *I have a new Tonka truck.*

He pointed a finger at me. "You have a soul. I can see it."

"Yeah," I said. "What's it look like?"

"It's fluffy and blue," he said. "My *favorite* color."

"Sorry," Margie said, pushing Superman into a metal seat. "Luke went to a church party yesterday over at First Methodist. I don't think he quite got the concept."

I remembered Luke from an article in the paper a few months back. He'd been a troubled kid—petty theft, drugs—on his way of making a career of it. Then he dove off Chimney rock and missed the water. His parents had some money, and they'd tried to take care of him at home when he got out of the hospital, until his little sister read him *Huck Finn,* and he rigged himself a raft out of an inner tube and tried to float down the Tallapoosa and nearly drowned. It took two days for the search party to find him. Misty, of course, cut the article out of the paper and pasted it in her journal, saying that sometimes we had to lose ourselves to find ourselves, which made about as much sense as most of what Misty said lately.

They'd set up the karaoke machine they used for their parties on a wooden stage, and I climbed up and did a few arm propeller movements and hip shakes to let them know the show was starting. As a nod to Luke, I opened with "Blue Moon," which Elvis recorded in his early years, when he was still raw and grainy, all his hurt close to the surface. *Blue moon, You saw me standing alone, Without a dream in my heart, Without a love of my own.*

Half the room just stared at me, and Sandy kept singing "Blackbird," and Margie was chasing some kid down the hall, but none of that mattered. I can't explain what happens to me when I perform, how everything sad in the world disappears, how I disappear. When I sing Elvis, I *am* Elvis. And I'm good.

When I finished the first number, the handful of people paying attention cheered, and Luke stomped his feet, and Kim yelled, " 'Lonesome Tonight'!" her face flushed, just like the shy housewives who used to go to Elvis's shows in their station wagons, dressed in their prim cardigans, and ended the night by tossing their bras onstage. That's the magic of Elvis. His music can transform anyone.

I sang "Are You Lonesome Tonight" for Kim, who swayed at the base of the stage, her eyes half-closed, and I wondered how she'd found her way to this town and this job, what she thought about when she climbed in her bed at night at the home, surrounded by strangers who worked her to the bone, some who couldn't even remember her name.

After I sang a few fast songs, I ended with "My Way," which

always makes me cry when I watch my video of Elvis performing it.

"Beautiful," Kim said with a sigh when I finished by falling to my knee, my head hung just so.

"That's uncanny, you being a girl and all," Margie said. "You sound just like him."

A little boy I hadn't noticed before was balled up in the corner, rocking himself. When I leaned over him and asked him if he wanted a *hunka hunka burnin' love,* he looked at me wild-eyed and shoved his hands over his ears.

"Don't take it personal," Margie said. "That's just what he does."

"What's wrong with him?" I said.

Kim was trying to usher everyone out onto the backyard patio, where they'd set up cookies and punch, and some of them danced a little jig out the door. I waved, and a few of the sharper ones waved back.

"As far as he knows, nothing," Margie said, lifting the boy, still curled in a knot, to her hip.

"You know," she said, "the moon really did turn blue once. I mean, I know that Elvis sings it like it's a symbol for lonely, but it was blue, truly, in the late 1800s. This Indonesian volcano exploded and messed everything up, turned sunsets green and the moon blue all around the world for the better part of two years."

For some reason, this made me sad, and when I got home, I told Misty what Margie had said, figuring if anyone could wrangle any meaning out of it, she could.

She was reading a historical romance, one of those Fabio

books with a white man pretending to be an Indian, a scrap of cow hide over his privates, a red feather tucked behind his ear the way a flamenco dancer wears a rose. She actually made notes in the margins but would never let me see what she wrote.

"Let me think on it," she said, scribbling something down in her journal.

Then I told her about the people at the home, Sandy's obsession with "Blackbird," Luke and his soul, the little boy who couldn't stand to hear the world.

"Do you think it's easier on them?" I said. "I mean, if you're slow enough that it's all softened a bit. The edge taken off."

"No," she said in a matter-of-fact way that meant she'd already thought about this exact question long and hard. "Most of them are just smart enough to know they've been cheated."

● ● ●

I woke up to find Misty sitting in the recliner next to my bed. She was dressed in her best curtain gown, long black velvet with arms so wide she looked like she had wings.

"Get dressed," she said. "And something nice. Not one of your Elvis getups."

"Where are we going?" I said, pulling off my nightgown. Misty turned her head so as not to see me naked. I'd always been a thin girl, and it hurt her, I think, to see what she wanted right in front of her every day.

"Have you ever been happy?" Misty said. "Truly happy. Because I can't ever remember being truly happy, which means something's wrong with me or the world, and I'm betting it's the world."

"Sure," I said. "The first time I ever performed."

Because she was a virgin and increasingly prudish, I didn't give her the details. One summer when I was barely fourteen, I biked to the local lake by myself, hid in a tiny cove, stripped naked, still not startled by my body, and sang while I bathed. How I understood love and pain and loneliness then. People think that childhood is good because you don't know, but it's not that you don't know, it's that you accept. An old man sliced into the cove in his fiberglass boat, his duct-taped rod arcing over the rim. I didn't stop singing or hide my breasts, and he didn't look scared or shocked or away. For a moment, I was nothing but voice.

"You're going to wear those?" Misty said when I slipped on some purple-sequined flip-flops that matched my sundress. She had on plain black pumps, the kind we wore in seventh grade.

"Sure," I said. "Why not?"

"Don't you ever take anything serious?" She looked pissed, which wasn't like Misty.

"How can I take something serious if I don't know what it is?" I said. "Where are we going, anyway?"

"Just meet me in the car," she said, and then stomped out of the room.

By the time I put on a little makeup and made it out to the driveway, Misty was sitting in her old Volvo with the motor running. When I opened the door, Clapton's "Promises" billowed out like an explosion. We would listen to it on repeat until we got out of the car. Misty was like that. She settled on a mood, and there was no budging her.

"My horoscope said I should expect change," Misty said as

we pulled out of the driveway. "A new journey. I thought maybe it meant that we should go on a trip. The beach or something. But then after journaling, I decided that a trip means you come back to exactly what you left. A journey means you are never again where you were before."

We passed by the Dairy Queen. A young family stood at the outside pickup counter waiting for their ice cream, the three of them holding hands and cooing at one another.

"You think they're *truly* happy?" I said. "That family back there?"

"Maybe," Misty said. "At least they have somebody."

"Maybe the wife's miserable," I considered. "Maybe the kid cries constantly. Tears up the house right after she's cleaned it. And maybe the husband's a freak. Makes her dress up like a schoolgirl or a nun or a schoolboy even. Maybe he whips her with the cord to the new power saw he bought instead of taking her on a vacation."

"What's your problem?" Misty said.

"Well, since my baby left me," I sang, "I've found a new place to dwell. It's down at the end of Lonely Street at Heartbreak Hotel."

This was the downside to impersonating. The day after the show, the world flooded back in, and I remembered who I was and where I was and how alone I was, and suddenly nothing seemed to matter much.

"Spare me," she said. "Most women would have killed for the husband you had."

Then she smoothed her hand over the droop of her belly. "I've lost weight," she said. "Ten pounds. I've been waiting for you to notice. Can you tell?"

"Sure," I lie. "You look great."

"Maybe it's just water weight," she says. "Maybe there's really no difference."

"No," I said. "Really. I can tell."

"Do you think they'll notice?"

"Do I think who will notice?"

"You know. Them." She gestured out the window toward the wide world.

We drove in silence for a while, just listening to music, and then Misty turned off on a dirt road and pulled up in front of a small white church.

"No way," I said. "No church for me. I've seen what it does to people, and I'm not going." Misty and I disagreed on many things, which was fine between old friends who couldn't remember a world without the other one in it, but one thing we'd always agreed on was to avoid joining the Jesus cult—not an easy task in a town like ours.

"I've been thinking about it for a while now, the meaning of things," Misty said. "They can't all be wrong. And they sure look a lot happier than I am."

"These people look happy to you?"

Old women in space-saucer-size hats were walking through the parking lot. Their faces stern, their lips pleated, as if they were marching off to their deaths, and for the life of me, I couldn't figure why they went each Sunday if it made them so miserable, except that some people like to be reminded of the virtue of suffering.

"This isn't the right one anyway," Misty said, pulling out of the parking lot. "I'll know when I find the right one."

We waited in the parking lot of five different churches, trying to get a glimpse of parishioners leaving the early service, because Misty said she wanted a church with soul. At the last church we went to, a small girl in braids and a ruffled dress was twirling on the church lawn, her patent-leather shoes gleaming, for a full five minutes. When she'd finally made herself drunk enough, she fell and stayed crouched on all fours, her white tights dirtied at the knees. Then she shot up, wiped the grit from her hands, and threw them into the air as if to say *Hallelujah*.

"This is the one," Misty said.

Who could have known that this would be the pivotal moment in Misty's life? That when we stood in the aisles of that church, arms swaying, voices lifted, *Why don't you swing down, sweet chariot, stop and let me ride,* and I knew exactly where I was, could smell the sweat on the woman in the lime green suit beside me, the sourness of her baby, could hear the kids swapping secrets from the balcony, the cars *swoosh*ing by, that Misty had left herself, that body she'd wanted to leave for so long, and finally found release.

"Wow," she said afterward, wiping the sweat from her neck, her hair springing in tight curls around her face. She looked breathless and blushed, completely in love.

When we got home, Misty went to the kitchen to put on some coffee, and I sat on the back porch and cracked open a beer.

"Beer," Misty said, walking out with two cups of coffee. "It's Sunday."

"Never bothered you before."

Across the street, the boys were loading Hubert Stringer into the hearse. Mr. Garret tipped his derby hat at us and waved.

"Did you know that Elvis almost gave everything up," Misty said, "all his fame and fortune, to join a gospel group because he felt the calling?"

"But he didn't."

"And look how he ended up." Misty nodded at the hearse.

"We all end up there sooner or later," I said. "I just bet Pearl Stringer thought it would be later."

"Henry called." Misty sat beside me. "There was a message on the machine."

"Fools rush in," I said, "where wise men never go."

"Will you stop with the Elvis lyrics. Don't you have anything original to say?"

"Why? He sang about everything that can be said."

"You should at least call," Misty said. "You should at least try to make it right."

Mr. Garret cranked up the hearse, off to take Hubert on his final tour before heading to the cemetery to be put in the ground next to Pearl, because whether he accidentally killed her or not, a wife's place was next to her husband in our town.

Months later, we would sit on the same porch, and a newly thin and engaged Misty, completely content and confident with her place in the world, would end our twenty-year friendship by asking the question she'd asked the morning she found God: "Have you ever been happy? Even for a moment? Because that's what I'm offering you." What she'd offered me was a reason to leave, and for that, I will always be grateful.

But for the time being, we sat peacefully in the heat of late afternoon, chatting about memories from our childhood, perhaps already grieving our unspoken loss, until night fell and the stars shone in the clouded sky and the moon rose high above us, the same moon that sometime, many years before me, decided that it did not want to be blue anymore and simply gave its color up.

rapture

The sky drapes low and dark, the shade of deep water before dawn, and Opal can't help thinking *Lord have mercy.* Her neighborhood is hushed. There are no children fighting or playing in yards, not a car flying by on the street too fast like they tend to do, just the sirens sounding sporadically throughout the morning.

Her husband, Glen, is somewhere in Georgia and Mother Winnie is at the Willow Springs Home and Opal is here and the new constellation of tornadoes is somewhere west and roiling this way. It is tornado season, and this happens, but something stirs different in Opal today, something that scares her in a way she cannot name, the voice in the back of her head whispering, *Now, the time is now,* and Mother Winnie there at the home, old and scared, surely, old and scared and alone unless you count nurses and caretakers, who don't count because they're not family.

"She'll be fine," Glen had said on the phone earlier

that morning. "You stay in the basement bathroom. You stay in the tub. You get yourself a flashlight and some water and a radio, and you stay there."

But Opal doesn't. Opal puts on a sundress, nice underwear, silk, in case the *now* she's hearing is a warning, a sign, and other hands will be undressing her, maybe in a hospital or a morgue or some field where her crumpled body lands after spinning and roiling in that constellation of tornadoes to the west and moving. She slips on strappy heels, applies lipstick the shiny, glossy red of a waxed apple. Then she takes the pie she made the night before from the fridge and heads for the car the weatherman on the radio and her husband and good sense have told her not to get in, and she drives the few miles through childless streets with dark sky draping low and everything different, some other world, to the Willow Springs Home, to Mother Winnie, who is Glen's mother but Opal's friend for the last twenty years, her married life.

The Tower, the nickname the tenants have given to the assisted living building in the Willow Springs retirement complex, is usually lively, old men playing cards or dominoes, the ladies in their mushroom caps of white hair, their cheeks overrouged, flirting with the old men or smoking on the patio and gossiping about children and grandchildren and church and one another, but everything is still, all seven floors of grimy windows cracked, the receptionist desk empty, the dinging of the elevator button when Opal pushes it startling.

Mother Winnie lives on the fourth floor, which is empty today, not a soul shuffling along, no breeze passing through the corridor to flutter the various photos of grandchildren or crayoned drawings of yellow suns and stick figures holding hands that tenants tape to their doors. But when Opal knocks on Mother Winnie's door and opens it, there is Mother Winnie, coiffed and powdered, dressed in a now too big, perfectly white suit, reclining in sullen lassitude on the burgundy velvet chaise longue she insisted be placed in her room. Tia, Mother Winnie's favorite caretaker, reads a fashion magazine on the bed. A radio sits in the window, and music Opal recognizes as her parents', as music from another time, plays tinny, merry.

"Ah, Opal!" Mother Winnie says. "How lovely of you to have brought pie."

"I told her to get herself to the basement with the others who can be moved, but she wouldn't have none of it," Tia says, flipping a shiny page. "What kind of pie you got?"

Tia is the only caretaker Mother Winnie will allow in the room without some type of verbal scuffle. "The girl's got style," Mother Winnie often says, "and for that, I'll forgive her transgressions." She likes the saucy shoes Tia wears with her uniform, even after she was chastised by the management.

"Chocolate." Opal sets the pie on the little table by the window showing flat dark sky. Mother Winnie is diabetic and is not supposed to have sugar, but she is also dying, dying so quickly, and Opal, right or wrong, tries to give the woman any pleasure she can, especially since Glen has kept so much joy from his mother these last few years.

"Yummy," Tia says, flipping another page. She has unbuttoned her uniform to her belly, and the dark globes of her breasts glisten in the heat of the day, the black lace of her bra scandalous in this small, low-rent retirement home apartment trying so hard not to look like the hospital room Opal knows it to be.

"Sit." Mother Winnie pats the chaise. "Have yourself a seat."

"Are you sure we shouldn't go on down to the basement?" Opal asks.

Mother Winnie snickers, says, "They always promise tornadoes in this part of the country, and I've yet to see one. Not one in eighty years, and if one comes, I'm seeing it."

Tia laughs, says, "Shit, nothing's going to get us. Nothing exciting ever happens at Willow Springs. Dying here, *that* you can count on, but not no fun way, not nothing that makes news." So Opal sits in a chair next to the window. She makes herself be as still as the day.

"I've been thinking," Mother Winnie says. "Red. I want you in red and nothing else. This is important." She throws herself back on the chaise, crosses rail-thin milky legs at the ankles, bats her eyes like a poster pinup girl. Things have been going this way for some months now, and it saddens Opal that her friend is slipping.

"Tia will be in green for obvious reasons," she says. "And me. Well of course, white. Nothing but white for me. It will be brilliantly metaphorical. We will slay them with our wit." Mother Winnie was a celebrated local poet in her day, until the poems became opaque and nonsensical, and not in a good way, until she began offering them as responses when spoken to at the grocery store or the post office, when asked simple questions, such as paper or plastic, priority or regular, until she couldn't separate the world from the page.

"Devastating," she's often said of everyone but herself.

"How these simple-minded people live their simple-minded lives."

"How about a piece of pie instead of a fashion revolution," Opal says, cutting wide wedges and plopping them on paper plates. She hands one to Tia and one to Mother Winnie, who stares at it for a moment, then takes a pink-nailed finger and pokes it into the viscous meat of the pie, keeps it there.

"The world has you pinned," Mother Winnie says. "You see? Pinned."

This is one metaphor of Mother Winnie's that Opal actually understands, and she smiles, handing a fork to the old woman, says, "Be good for me today, okay? I'm tired, you know. Very tired."

"Well, of course you are," Mother Winnie says, shoving pie into her mouth. "That's the way they want you."

"She's a handful, isn't she," Tia says, her red pumps dangling from each big toe off the side of Mother Winnie's bed. "You should have heard what she told me to do with my boyfriend to get things fired up again when we thought he might've been wandering." The idea that anyone would cheat on young, glorious Tia is hard for Opal to comprehend.

"Bastards," Mother Winnie says.

"Bastards," Tia says.

"We should go to the basement," Opal repeats.

"Where's the booze?" Mother Winnie says. "Isn't this a party? Camille will be here in no time, and we best toast to her." Mother Winnie does not realize that she's conflated decades of time, as she often does these days, and Opal will not mention it, will not ruin the festive mood.

There is a picture of a younger Mother Winnie on Opal's bedside table at home, a large home built for babies that never came. The picture is of Mother Winnie during Hurricane Camille in 1969. Mother Winnie and a group of her friends refused to leave their historic Gulf homes and threw a party instead, a party like no other. The picture was taken on a screened-in porch, and surely the violence of nature is in the background, somewhere all of that destruction is going on, but Mother Winnie, she lies across a couch, her hip cocked, creamy arms exposed in a gauzy shirt, her mouth puckered around smoke rings, a cigarette dangling from a gesturing hand, a sweating drink in the other. She is talking to someone—perhaps Glen's father, perhaps a friend, perhaps a lover, perhaps the storm itself. She looks angry or in love, Opal cannot tell which. "Rapture" is the word she uses to describe the look on Mother Winnie's face, and that word, Opal thinks, embraces anger and love.

"No alcohol," Opal says, and she says it carefully, under her breath, bracing herself for Mother Winnie's response, whose list of health problems includes alcoholism, although no one ever gives it that name, exactly. Tia hunkers down on the bed, her plate of pie on her flat belly, and lifts the magazine she's reading over her face to hide.

"Where's Omar? Where is he? He'll fetch us some cocktails." Mother Winnie has sat up, a struggle, her body shaking with the sickness that her beauty and attitude hide so well. She is about to weep, convincingly. Opal knows the drill.

"Omar's dead, Mother Winnie," Opal says.

In fact, Omar has been dead for over five years. And if he were here, indeed he would fetch Mother Winnie anything she wanted, because that's exactly what he did for fifty years in spite of or because of Mother Winnie's infidelities and other smaller cruelties, and Glen hates his mother for it.

Opal knows Mother Winnie met Omar, Glen's father, in the war, that she was a nurse, their affair spanning continents. That Winnie had thought Omar had been shot down over some island in the Philippines, that she was told as much, that she married another soldier, impulsively, out of grief, and that man actually did get shot down, which Winnie saw in some ways as a blessing. Omar's death, the real one, wasn't nearly as romantic as the false one. He suffered a stroke five years before while mowing the lawn for the Labor Day barbecue, fell off his prized riding lawn mower, dangling there like a wounded Indian on a horse in a bad western.

"Can you believe it," Glen had said. "Now we will always associate Labor Day with Pop's death."

Opal had to try hard not to laugh at her husband's somber sentiments, an urge she could not understand, an urge she prayed would stop. For Opal, it was the beginning of something, a shift in their marriage Glen never noticed.

"I need a drink," says Mother Winnie, who has surprised both Opal and Tia by not weeping. "And you," she says to Opal, mouth full of pie, "you need a lover. It's time. Your thirties—it's perfect. Glen leaves you alone too much. He'd want you to be happy. I raised him that way, raised him to please a woman."

"I'm forty-five," Opal says.

Mother Winnie coughs on her pie, and both Tia and Opal lean into the old woman instinctively. "Good God," Mother Winnie says, "when did you get so old?"

"What could a little drink hurt?" Tia asks—Tia, who is too young to know much hurt. And suddenly Opal, who does not drink, needs a drink herself, badly.

The weatherman occasionally interrupts the music on the radio sitting in the window showing flat black sky, says the threat is still some distance away but coming closer, ever closer, and Opal can feel it distinctly, in this room with them, this room she has to get out of *now,* the voice says.

So she leaves Mother Winnie and Tia to their pie and magazines and music, walks down the dingy empty corridor, takes the elevator to the unmanned lobby, gets back into the car the weatherman on the radio and her husband and good sense have told her to stay out of, and drives the few miles through the still streets of their small Gulf town to the local market to buy beer or wine or both.

The parking lot is carless. Nothing stirs in it. Not a plastic bag rustling. The air is that heavy.

There's a lone cashier smoking a cigarette behind his register, although surely that cannot be allowed in a grocery store, not in this day and age, but there he is, smoking and smiling, the normal classical music that hums in the background replaced with something loud and metal, a sound Opal hears coming from cars packed with raucous teenagers. The music is relentless, following Opal down each aisle as she gathers cheese and crackers and wine and beer and milk in case she changes her mind and decides not to drink because she's really not a drinker. In front of the checkout aisle is a display of disposable cameras, and on impulse, Opal grabs one, shoves it into her plastic basket, because she wants a picture, a picture of her facing a storm, a picture of her like the one of Mother Winnie on her bedside table.

"Hi," Opal says to the cashier as she hands him her basket of groceries. His name tag says "Rat." When the boy doesn't respond, simply begins scanning her groceries, a cigarette dangling from his mouth, she says, "Some weather we're having, Rat," and he pauses for a moment, his face slick with its overproductive glands, his eyes angry because she's there, interrupting his private concert, and he doesn't answer, doesn't have to pretend to be interested or jovial, because it's Opal and Rat only, no one else to monitor their interaction. And Opal is so angry, Mother Winnie sick and slipping, Glen somewhere in Georgia, always somewhere else, disaster roiling its way toward them, and this boy not caring or understanding or pretending to be kind. It's all she can do not to leap across the counter, not to take that cigarette and put it out on his pitifully adolescent face.

"Thirty-two fifty," he says, blowing smoke out of the corner of his mouth.

Opal hands him two twenties, and he puts them both in the register, shuts it.

"My change?" she says, eyeing her groceries, which from the look of things Rat has decided not to bag.

"No change," he says, lighting another cigarette. "I don't have change, and there's no one here to open another register or make some change." He smiles, blows smoke out of the corner of his mouth like Rat does, says, "I can write you a note. An IOU."

But by now Opal is shoving her cheese and crackers and wine and beer and milk and camera into a paper bag herself, and she is thinking, What has this world come to? She stomps out of the local market in her strappy sandals without looking at Rat, without acknowledging his existence, a rude impulse she would never have indulged before, no matter what the circumstances, never before this day, when things are different.

She trudges over to her car that she knows better to get into but doesn't care enough not to, the car she half hopes the roiling tornadoes that seem nothing more than a false promise will pluck up with their whipping tails, dropping her in some other world where things are peaceful and kind and rearranged.

And this is what she's thinking—scaring herself, really, because wishing such things might make them happen, so she's thinking these things and apologizing to God at the same time—when there's a knock on her car window, and Opal realizes she's not alone in the once empty parking lot of the local market, that there's a smiling man tapping on her window, a smiling man mouthing something to her.

Opal rolls down her window without thinking, stupid Opal, she will think later, and finds a gun in her face, just like on TV but real. The man behind the gun says, "Don't say a word, bitch, just get out of the car," and certainly this cannot be the world in which Opal lives.

"May I get my groceries?" she asks without knowing she's going to ask it, although in an hour she will tell herself that she did, that she thought it through. But she asks because her purse is in that bag and she needs it, and surprisingly, the man says yes, perhaps because he is not experienced at such things as stealing cars from aging women. Then her car and the man are gone, and Opal stands alone in the parking lot in her sundress with her groceries and without her car or a description of the man who took it. It's as if she never saw him.

She walks to the pay phone placed so close to the front of the store that if she stands too far to the left, the mechanized doors open and close rhythmically like a landed fish gulping. The sky has not changed. There are no cars on the road to stop and ask for help. Rat is no longer standing in front of his register, smoking, listening to his private concert.

"Are you in danger?" the dispatcher at the local police station asks when Opal calls in the robbery.

And Opal thinks, I don't know, am I? Are we? But she says, "No, I don't think so." And the dispatcher, not unkindly, tells Opal that things are crazy, just insane, that every wacko has come out from under his rock because of the tornadoes, that a car theft is not top priority. She gives Opal the name and number of the only cab company in town and tells her to come to the station tomorrow. Tomorrow she can file a report.

"We're busy, very busy," the man at the cab company says. "It might be ten minutes, it might be an hour. I really can't say."

Opal sits on the edge of the sidewalk in front of the market with her groceries and waits. The sky drapes low and black. She could call Glen, who is in Georgia on business, a pharmaceutical rep who makes good money, who provides them with a good life. But what could he do except worry? So she sits, pulls a beer from the groceries she bagged herself, opens it, takes a bitter swallow, then pours the rest out, piss yellow, on the black asphalt.

Things begin to look up, things begin to go Opal's way, she thinks, when the cab she called swerves into the parking lot and stops in front of her. She peeks into the passenger-side front door to greet the cabdriver, and she's so thankful for a moment, so thankful!—until she realizes the cab is almost full, two bodies in the back, one in the front passenger seat, then the driver.

"Hi," she says, sliding over cracked vinyl into the back next to a graying man her age, trying to balance her groceries in her lap, trying not to let her thigh brush against the hard thigh of the man. To his left, a large, robust woman in a floral muumuu, age indiscernible, holds a toy poodle in her barely lap. Neither dog nor woman makes a peep, they just stare at the back of the cabbie's head. In the passenger seat, a young woman in a silver miniskirt, blond and tanned, has her legs stretched over the glove compartment.

"Isn't this wild?" she says to Opal or no one in particular. In the driver's seat hunches a black man, who is scowling for good reason.

"Things are crazy," the cabdriver says. "The world gone mad. Where you going?"

Opal realizes that she cannot go back to Willow Springs because she no longer has a car, that she must go home without providing Mother Winnie and Tia with their cocktails, and this disappoints her, because there won't be many more days with Mother Winnie, and certainly never another day such as this. And there won't be a picture of her like the one she has of Mother Winnie, a picture of her throwing caution to the wind, literally. A picture of her facing the relentlessness of nature and fate with a smile and a drink. She gives the cabbie her address, and he tells her she's the last to be dropped off and drives in the opposite direction of her home, even though it's barely two miles away.

The cabbie cranks the radio, echoing the concerns of the weatherman who says the tornadoes are coming for sure with a "*Praise Jesus,*" with a "*God help us all.*"

"Don't talk," whispers the man sitting next to her. "He gets angry if he can't hear the radio."

"That's right," the cabbie says. "I get angry because my ass is the one driving you around with the whole sky going to fall. It ain't right working me on a day like today. And the minute they say tornadoes are here, my ass is out of this car, I don't care where on God's green earth we are."

"See," the man whispers, his breath minty, pleasant, his leg pressed into hers no matter how far she scoots toward the door.

"You don't see nothing," the cabbie says, turning to look at them as he speaks, looking at them and not the empty road. His eyes are bulbous and dark, the whites tinged yellow, and Opal tries not to gasp. She looks out the window at the sky the radio announcer swears will collapse in an hour, maybe two, maybe over and over again all afternoon and night as constellations of tornadoes form and roil their way. And Opal thinks that God is punishing her for the thoughts she had while sitting in the parking lot of that empty market, punishing her for the thoughts she has about her husband, who is never home because he works so hard, tries so hard to provide them a good life, punishing her for what they've done to Mother Winnie, who is too far gone to remember.

"We're here," the cabbie says, and Opal looks at where they are and has no idea as to where "here" is. They are in a part of town she never drives in, even though their town is small, because Glen always points down the road where Opal has now been, points down the road and says, Don't ever, ever go there, especially by yourself, and in the twenty years of her married life, she never has until this day when things are different.

The large woman who does not speak pulls bills from her purse, hands them to the cabbie, then lurches out of the cab, her poodle tucked under a fleshy arm, toward a row of tiny houses, shacks really, grassless yards made of pine needles and sand, yards full of aluminum cans and derelict cars and plastic toys and rubber balls, but no children, and Opal feels shamed that she lives in such a large house on the other side of town, a house bigger than all these shacks put together, a house built for babies that never came.

"You can scoot over," Opal says to the man next to her, who has not moved to occupy the space where the large woman once sat.

"Thank you," he says, "but I prefer it here."

"I swear," says the girl in the front with her long tan legs spread over the console, her silver skirt pushed so far up her young thighs that there's nothing left not to see, "this weather is fucking wild."

"Shhh," the cabbie says, cranking the radio even louder, and the weatherman advises listeners to stay out of cars, to find a safe place, a basement, a bathroom, a ditch, that tornadoes have touched down thirty miles to the west and are coming here, that they should be here any minute. "God forgive us," the cabbie says, pressing his foot on the accelerator, spinning on wet pine needles, and the cab swerves farther down the road Opal has never been on before this day, her groceries cold on her lap, the man's thigh hot on hers.

They stop in front of another row of shacks, and the tan blond girl unwinds her legs from atop the console, leans into the cabbie, presses her fat lips against his dark, thin cheek, says, "I'll catch you later, Jerome, baby," and leaves the cab without paying. Then the sirens start, a nuclear fallout, the end of the world, *now,* the voice in Opal's head says.

"Get out," Jerome says, pulling his keys from the ignition. "Everyone get out now."

"Here?" Opal asks, never having been here before.

"Here's as good a place not to die as any, lady," Jerome says, getting out of the cab. "I'll take you home when it's over. You meet me here when it's over." Then he disappears into the same shack the blond girl sashayed into just moments before.

"C'mon," says the man sitting next to her, "we'll go to Frankie's. It's just around the corner." He politely takes Opal's groceries, his arm grazing her breasts as he scoops them up, and they slide out of the cab into the dark day, which has grown even darker. The sun had begun to set, the sky now tinged with a putrid gold, the color of pus.

Opal tries to balance in her strappy sandals while walking through sandy dirt and pine needles farther down the road. She thinks to make small talk but has never talked to anyone such as the man walking next to her in an aged old-fashioned suit, a bow tie, his graying hair gelled back, his smile sparkly in a way that is friendly or dangerous.

"So," Opal says, smoothing her wrinkled sundress over her hips. "What's your name?"

"Gabe," the man says, her bag of groceries under one strong arm.

"What a lovely name!" Opal says, deciding this she can do, small pleasantries are her forte. And things would be better once they got to Frankie's, where they would be safe, even though Opal has no idea who or what Frankie is. "I'm Opal."

"A pleasure," Gabe says.

He stops in front of a rickety door to an even more rickety wooden building with a Bud Light sign flickering in the filthy window. "This is Frankie's."

Frankie's, of course, is a bar, and not one of the nice clubs Glen sometimes takes Opal to on their anniversary or after a promotion. This bar has signed dollar bills stapled all over the walls, mismatched bras and panties hanging from wooden beams, the concrete floor covered in cigarette butts and ashes and peanut shells. The place is packed with the kind of people that if Opal saw walking behind her on the sidewalk, she would hug her purse closer, cross to the other side, her heart full of fear, her heart full of guilt because of her fear, for thinking such things simply because the people looked poor, which is no indicator of character, no matter what Glen says.

"Frankie!" Gabe says to the round, round bartender in a dirty white T-shirt, both hands gripping cans of beer.

"Gabe!" Frankie says.

Then Gabe sets Opal's bag of groceries on the counter and asks Frankie to pop them in the fridge for the lady while they wait out the storm, and Opal reaches into her bag and grabs her purse and her camera, just in case there is a chance for a picture in this place she should never, never go alone on this day she should be cowering in her basement, in her tub, with a flashlight and a radio and a gallon of water.

Frankie pushes two glasses of liquor toward them, liquor the pus color that now tinges the sky, says, "On the house," then takes Opal's groceries and heads somewhere behind an old sheet that serves as a door to what Opal presumes is the storeroom. The radio is tuned to the tornado report as if it were a football game, and occasionally someone cheers, says, *Bring it on, baby!* and others cheer and toasts are made.

Luckily enough, there is an empty booth in the back of the bar near the signs for the bathrooms, and Gabe gallantly waves toward the seat, says, "Ladies first." Opal slides in, and Gabe follows, opting to sit next to her instead of across the booth.

"So," Gabe says, "what's a lady such as yourself doing out on a day such as this?"

Opal notices he is handsome, strikingly so, if a bit worn, and his smile is indeed kind, not dangerous, surely not any more danger in one day, so she dimples in a way she hasn't dimpled since she can remember, says, "I was out grabbing a few things for my mother-in-law," then worries about Mother Winnie, whom she has forgotten about until this moment. Dying Mother Winnie, who Glen hates, who Glen forced into that terrible home with the misnomer Willow Springs no matter how much Opal begged, no matter that they could afford much better, that they could have brought her to their huge home built for babies that never came, because he hates his mother, hates what she did to his father, even though his father loved Mother Winnie, understood her, and loved all of her in a way Opal now understands Glen will never love her.

"What a kind, thoughtful daughter-in-law you are," Gabe says, patting her thigh and keeping his hand there.

"Well, thank you," Opal says, and the bar cheers at the radio, and everyone toasts, including Opal, who chokes on liquor she never drinks. Immediately her head is warm, her leg hot under Gabe's hand.

"So what do you do with yourself on normal days unlike this?" Gabe asks, inching his hand higher, and they both take another sip from their drinks.

What does Opal do? Opal plants tomatoes in the backyard, tulips and sunflowers and petunias, which is what Glen calls her, Petunia, and there are worse things to be called. She gardens, has tea with friends, spends afternoons with Mother Winnie when Glen is out of town, which is always. She invites women over to talk about books with female characters who do similar things until one day their lives are changed by this or that.

"I'm a housewife," Opal says.

Gabe's hand moves higher up her skirt. "What a noble pursuit," he says, tweaking his bow tie. "Every woman should be so noble. Should stay at home with her children."

"No children," Opal says. "It wasn't in God's plan." It was in Glen's plan that they should have a household of children, that she should stay home, that a wife's place is in the home, not gallivanting about town reciting indecent poetry to glazed-eyed lovers, and when it was understood that Opal would never get pregnant, it was also understood that she would still stay at home.

"A picture," Gabe says. "We should commemorate this day

with a picture." He grabs the disposable camera off the table, hands it to a frizzy-haired woman tripping drunk out of the bathroom, says, "Would you mind?"

And the sirens sound again, or something like a siren, something loud like a train thundering too close, and the woman takes the camera, says, "Cheese!" The flash startles Opal, whose skirt is around her waist now, Gabe's delicate hands fingering the edge of the silk panties she wore in case other hands undressed her in a hospital or a morgue or some field where her crumpled body lands after spinning and roiling in the constellation of tornadoes here, here right now in this part of town where Opal should never, never go alone.

The woman sets down the camera and picks up Gabe's drink, and someone yells, *Bring it on, baby!* She downs his drink, the small bar shaking from wind, the day no longer still or quiet. Opal's heart is in her throat, and Gabe's long, delicate finger is in her, under the table, with everyone cheering. Something comes alive inside of her, moving, a darkness in her belly hung low.

And then it is still again. Quiet. Everyone grumbling, *Is that all you have?* The weatherman saying that rain will follow, torrential rain, rain like they have never seen before.

"It's over?" Opal asks. "That's it?" Somehow, she's disappointed.

"Will you excuse me?" Gabe says, smiling, removing his finger, smoothing Opal's skirt down over her legs. He stands and disappears into the back under the bathroom signs.

Opal decides that when Gabe gets back from the bathroom, she will offer herself to him. She will go to whatever shack he might live in, and she will spread herself naked and give herself over. She'll do things she never does with Glen, things she only reads about in books she talks about with women who have never done them, either.

Only the rain comes, as harsh as the weatherman promised, and Gabe doesn't return. After twenty minutes, Opal begins to worry, begins to think about what has happened, this strange man, inside of her!, this bar full of the kind of people with whom she never speaks, except to say paper or plastic, priority or regular. She worries that maybe Jerome the cabbie has left, and how will she get home, who will she call?

So she shoves the camera in her purse, leaves the groceries somewhere behind that sheet that serves as a door to the storeroom at Frankie's bar, and begins the walk back to the cab, the day now night, the rain as relentless as the metal music in the local market some other lifetime ago, and thank God, the cab is there, Jerome in it, just as he promised.

"The Lord's decided to spare us," Jerome says. "You never know what He'll decide."

And naturally, Opal begins to cry, because what has she become, who is she now?

"Come now," Jerome says. "No need to be scared of a little rain. The tornadoes have passed, and we're going to get you home and safe."

They ride silently through the flooding streets, no children fighting or playing in yards, not a car flying by too fast, the dispatcher buzzing on and off, on and off, until finally Jerome slaps at the buttons on the radio, their lights flickering out, and turns into the driveway. Opal smiles, says, "Thank you so, so much," thinking he deserves a huge tip, a reckless tip, Glen would say, for waiting on her, for taking her home to her large house, so big and empty, and she gives it all to him, every last cent in her wallet. When she opens her purse to slip the wallet back in, she notices that the disposable camera is gone.

"Please," she says to Jerome, "wait just a moment longer." She searches under the seats, beside the doors, squeezes her hands down any crevice she can find. The camera is gone, and there is nothing to be seen but the back of Jerome's head and the wet sky draping low and dark. There would be no proof, no revelation of the kind of woman she could have been given the right circumstances, no picture of her facing the relentlessness of nature and fate with a smile and a drink, just the memory of a strange man's hand quivering at the hem of her skirt in a bar on a road where she should never, never have gone alone. And Opal thinks that maybe this is a kind of punishment, a reminder that what's done in one's life cannot be undone or transformed by sheer will into something kinder, and how cruel, she thinks, that the Lord would have so little mercy.

So she gets out of the cab and walks toward the house, a house bigger than all those shacks with grassless yards made of pine needles and sand put together, and she's at the front door before she realizes that she no longer has her keys, that her keys are in the hands of some smiling thief who at this moment could be driving her car in some other town; so she pulls the spare house key from under the straw mat on their front step offering a merry WELCOME, the key they always keep there because that's the kind of neighborhood they live in.

She steps into her home and right there, in the foyer, removes the dress Gabe slid up her thighs, the panties he caressed with those long, delicate fingers. She removes her dress and panties and her strappy sandals and walks naked and shamed to the guest bath, not wanting to see herself in the floor-length mirror in the master bath, and she showers a very long time. Then she finds the most modest nightgown she owns, and there are many modest nightgowns to choose from, and she puts it on and slides into her bed and listens to the rain, which grows louder and louder, the shutters on her windows trembling, the sky shaking with thunder and lightning, angry almost, and Opal weeps and Opal prays and finally Opal sleeps with the light on, because she is that scared.

Sometime in the middle of the night, the light goes out, and Opal wakes, her heart again in her throat, and everything like a bad hangover she's never had floods back to her. The room is so dark, she cannot see her hand in front of her face. She crawls out of bed, feeling her way toward the window where the shutters were trembling earlier but are now silent, no rain, no wind, and she peels back the drapes to the blackest night she's ever seen, not a streetlight on, not a light in a neighbor's home, not a star, not a moon, nothing but lifeless black. *Now,* the voice in her head says, *now.* And she understands what this moment is, what is happening to her while on her knees in an empty house. That it is *now,* the end, the moment when babies are taken from their cribs, their sinful mothers left behind, the rapture descending upon them like a thief in the night. Only Opal has no babies to disappear, no babies to leave her behind, so she weeps because she is uncertain about many things, not noticing the front door opening, not noticing footsteps walking toward her bedroom.

Then the bedroom door opens and a voice says, "Opal," so softly. She cannot tell who the voice belongs to, if perhaps it is her own, but she understands that judgment is upon her all the same.

pilgrimage in georgia

Louis and Esther Peter discovered Blyght, Georgia, by accident when Louis made a wrong turn on their way to a writers conference in Atlanta. Louis had insisted on taking the back roads in order to experience the countryside, the barely populated towns where he said real people lived. "These are my people," he'd said somewhat defensively to Esther, who, accustomed to Louis's frequent indulgences in melancholia, simply pointed to her watch.

Blyght wallowed in decay: crumbling false-front buildings, graying white-columned homes in the "good" section of town. It sported a Kimmie's Fine Dining and a Piggly Wiggly and a Bill's Dollar Store, which had $1 old-fashioned panties staked like tents in the window. A spray-painted tiger, the high school mascot, leapt from the water tower, and Louis knew, because he just knew, that on Friday nights after the football games, some teenager got arrested for trying to climb to the top to get drunk and naked. It was the kind of town Louis wrote about, the kind he grew up in, and it stirred in him a nostalgia that made him want to unlearn himself.

They stopped at Kimmie's diner and ate salty cubed steak and green beans cooked to mush with ham hocks and doughy biscuits to sop it all up, while blond, permed Kimmie sat at the lunch counter watching TV, her face pushed dangerously close to the oscillating fan.

"Where y'all from?" she asked when she wandered over to their table to top off their teas.

"Not far from here," Louis answered, and she shot him a slightly skeptical look.

"Chicago," Esther said. "We've lived in Chicago for some years now."

"I bet you don't get beans like that in Chicago." Kimmie slipped their ticket onto the table. "Snapped them myself," she said before moving on to another one of the few occupied tables, a sweating pitcher of tea cradled against her plump abdomen.

"Isn't she beautiful?" Louis whispered to Esther, who sighed, then offered him a ten-minute lecture on the dangers of romanticizing poverty in literature and country-western songs.

"Have you lost your mind?" she said finally, picking the ham fat out of her beans. "It's so sad here."

"Look around, Esther," Louis said. "Really look."

A few feet away, an older, pink-faced man in work overalls quietly sipped soup from his spoon. A woman, presumably his wife, in a sweatshirt stenciled with a dancing bear sat across from him, sawing patiently at a pear with her fork.

Esther appeared confused, as if she were staring at one of those optical illusion posters full of dots, the kind that if you just focus hard enough, a beautiful butterfly or dove or something of the kind emerges like magic.

• • •

One year to the day after their first foray into Blyght, and several years before March Gayle Dewlittle showed up on their front porch looking for literary guidance, Louis and Esther moved to Blyght in order to inspire authenticity (his words) in their lives and in his writing.

Although originally from Georgia, Louis had taught fiction for two decades at a small prestigious university in Chicago. But, having succeeded in the academic world, so to speak, he was in a position where he no longer had to teach. Instead, he served occasionally as a keynote speaker at writers conferences, where he discussed such pertinent topics as landscape as metaphor, how inanimate objects convey emotion, how a front porch may serve as a symbol of the soul, how to make a weeping willow or collapsed bridge speak the universal.

He hadn't published a word in almost seven years.

At dinner parties and author receptions with colleagues in Chicago, Louis would drink one glass of boxed wine too many, then hiss to Esther about the banality of it all. How could he be expected to write anything in this academic wasteland?

Esther, a doctor's daughter from Atlanta, had grown to like Chicago. In a fit of middle-aged academic revival, she took classes at the university where Louis taught. She had friends who knew the names of philosophers and designers of handbags, the subtle differences between Armadale and Stoli. She had been persuaded to move to Blyght only because of its proximity to her family, whom Louis had promised to visit on requisite holidays, birthdays, and so forth.

The first time someone at MK's bar, the only bar in Blyght, asked him how he had ended up moving to the town, Louis, with much fanfare, explained that on the evening of his retirement party at the university, he and Esther, more than a little tipsy, opened a map of the Southeast on their bed and made love gliding over the Appalachians, the Mississippi, the mouth of the Gulf. They'd agreed that wherever the wet spot landed was where they would move. He ended the tale by saying, "And here we are," his hand and shoulders lifted into a shrug. Obviously this was an unbelievable story, except for the part about the retirement party, which did happen at one time, and at which Louis did get drunk, and after which Esther had to make several apologetic phone calls citing Louis's vulnerability; but this was the story that Louis told, and the group of men at the bar howled, said, *"That Louis is all right,"* patting him and one another on the shoulder while Louis bought everyone a round.

"This is honest," he said to his new friends late in the evening. "This is pure."

"*Sure thing,*" they said.

• • •

Louis discovered Scooter Light at the Blyght library a week after he and Esther had settled into their new home, an old barn that had been converted into a split-level a decade before. Esther kept herself busy decorating it while Louis spent his days wandering about town, picking conversations with strangers, or checking out books from the tiny, red-brick library, which he knew carried two of his earlier titles because he'd looked—beautifully designed books from well-respected academic publishers. Now, when he held them so many years later, the clouded Mylar wrapper seemed to mute the possibility the books promised when first published.

Louis saw Scooter at the library daily, a gaunt young man dressed in jeans and a T-shirt pacing in front of the library with a strange sense of purpose, his chest pitched forward like a bird dog catching a scent. Often he'd mumble what he read while pacing, ash his cigarette in a brisk, clean motion. Louis would sit in the coolness of the library, crouched in the kiddie reading nook because it was by the window, his body folded into a primary yellow plastic chair. He would sit this way and watch.

"Who's that?" Louis asked the librarian as she shelved books in his reading nook. She wore her copper-colored hair in the helmet style of old ladies, although she couldn't have been more than forty, and if she thought it bizarre that Louis sat in the kiddie nook, she kept it to herself.

"Scooter Light," she said, touching her fingers to her thin upper lip. Louis noticed she did this often when anyone spoke directly to her.

"What's he reading?"

"Who knows. He never checks them out from the library." Behind her hung a faded poster of a kid with his mouth open, boldfaced words marching down his throat. **Feed your head!** it ordered. **Read!**

Soon Louis began positioning himself on the bench in

front of the library before Scooter arrived. He brought bad Chevron coffee and a book he never managed to read. Scooter would nod at Louis as he lurched up the walkway, and Louis would nod in return. Then Scooter would tap a cigarette from the inexplicably crisp pack he kept in his back pocket, fish a book out of an old cloth sack he carried over his shoulder, and commence to read and ash. This went on for days, and Louis felt like a literary version of a scientist in the jungle waiting to earn the trust of the gorillas.

"What are you reading?" Louis asked after a week or so.

Scooter stopped pacing, stared at the book in his hands as if surprised to find it there, then looked directly at Louis for the first time, his eyes strangely owl-like, the skin beneath them tinged the color of mud.

He closed the book on his finger to mark his place, then poked the spine toward Louis almost shyly.

Louis squinted, trying to read the title, but without his glasses, he couldn't make out the gold lettering.

"Ahh," Louis said. "Great book."

"You've read it?" Scooter asked. "I thought I was the only one around here who liked Zoline."

"Oh no," Louis said. "I've read it several times. He's great."

Scooter stared at him for a moment, his great owl eyes wide and unblinking, then he smiled, nodded at Louis, opened the book, and began reading and pacing all over again.

Louis was surprised but pleased when a few afternoons later Scooter put out his cigarette on the bottom of his boot, tossed his book into his sack, and walked straight up to him, standing there awkwardly for a moment before saying, "I drink bourbon."

At first, Louis thought the comment some strange type of a bumper sticker declaration, like GOD IS MY CO-PILOT or I DIG DRUNK CHICKS, before it dawned on him that this was Scooter's way of asking him to have a drink.

"I love bourbon," Louis said. And he did love bourbon, but Esther forbade him to drink it since an incident in Chicago, which involved him weeping at a dinner party. She said it made him maudlin.

They walked down to MK's bar, slid into a cracked vinyl booth, and ordered drinks from the proprietor, Mick, a hunched-over octogenarian, who patted Scooter's shoulder after writing down their order.

When Scooter asked Louis why he'd moved to Blyght, Louis told him his story about the map, and Scooter grinned, his lip pulled up on the right side, as if a string were tugging there.

"I thought you might have been, you know, funny." Scooter fluttered his hand in the air.

"Oh, I watch everybody," Louis said.

When Louis asked Scooter what he did with his days, Scooter said he cut grass here and there and wrote down little stories to amuse himself.

"Really?" Louis said. He hadn't expected this, Scooter writing, and he felt a flash of nervous nausea.

"What do you write?" Louis asked, relaxing, because he figured that Scooter, who had on jeans and a Hooters T-shirt, was probably the kind to write bad crime mysteries whose supposed eloquence made some doe-eyed redneck girl in electric blue eyeliner swoon. He imagined impromptu writing sessions over a stained table at Kimmie's diner. After an afternoon of blackberry cobbler, bad coffee, and intense writing, they would share their work. Louis would say something insightful. And when Louis presented his work to Scooter, the young man would stare at him with those unblinking eyes, take off the inevitable CAT cap he wore, rake a hand through his misshapen curls, and say something simple but huge, like *WOW.*

"Nothing special," Scooter replied, dipping his hands deep into his jeans pockets. "Just town stories, secrets and pilfering and such."

After a few drinks, Scooter revealed that his first novel had come out just months before. This revelation irritated Louis, who had thought of himself as the only writer-in-residence of Blyght.

Louis tried to find a way to work it into the conversation that he himself was a writer.

"No kidding," Scooter said when Louis finally managed to mention his best-received book, *A Pilgrimage in Georgia.* "I've read it."

"Really," Louis said.

"Yeah," Scooter said. "It was something else."

"You think?"

"Sure thing." Scooter turned toward the bar, signaled to the octogenarian to bring two more drinks.

"Anything you liked in particular?" Louis felt desperate, like a pimply boy at a dance.

"Oh, lots of stuff. Lots of things for sure."

• • •

When Louis went home that evening, he excused himself from dinner by saying he had a voice in his head that had to be put to paper and examined the advance praise on the back cover of the reviewers' copy of a *Dog's Day Night* Scooter had pulled from his cloth sack and offered to Louis before they'd left the bar.

Raw and relentless and flawless. Strong, grim, haunting, a work of terrible beauty rendered in muscular prose.

Voice as straight and true as the barrel of a Remington. This novel burns.

Cuts to the bone. Lay your money down and buy this book.

If Carson McCullers and James Dickey had a lovechild, his name would be Scott Light. Spectacular debut by the most original southern voice in a decade.

Scooter? Scooter Light the most original southern voice? Raw? Muscular prose?

"What do you care?" Esther said that night in bed as she thumbed through a Crate & Barrel catalog and watched a rerun of a talk show. "You've outlasted thirty years of up-and-comers. Go to sleep."

She stared at the TV a few moments, its colors flickering over the soft curves of her face, and then she spoke the unspeakable, quietly, lying on the red bedspread of their redundantly red bedroom—red carpet, red drapes, red lamp shades, all the shade of a barn—her still-slim ankles crossed.

"Louis," she said, "do you miss him? Do you think that's

why you're never content?" The accusation in her voice was obvious, the slight puffs of flesh at the corners of her mouth sullen.

"Who?" he said. He'd spent fifteen years avoiding conversations with Esther about his ex-wife and son, and it irritated him that she would pick now, of all times, to bring it up.

"Who do you think?" she said, annoyed, flipping the channels.

"No," he said.

On the TV, a talk show host told an obese woman that she was fat because she wanted to be invisible. "Are you ready to be seen?" the host whispered into the microphone, her eyes blue and grave. The camera cut to the fat woman, who wept, her chins quaking.

"Sometimes I think it's my fault you left them," Esther said. "Sometimes I think I'm being punished for it. Sometimes I think I'm evil." She rubbed the web of indigo veins on her left temple, and Louis kissed her there.

They sat in silence.

"But Scooter's an idiot," Louis blurted out. "A hack." He could not stop thinking about it, what this meant, could not wrap his mind around the idea of Scooter the phenom.

"Have you read his book?"

"I don't have to read his book," Louis said, and immediately felt exposed, and he resented Esther for witnessing it.

"Have you ever stopped to think about how parasitic writing is?" Esther said. "I've been thinking about it a lot lately, how it's nothing more than feeding off others' lives. Have you thought about that?"

"I just don't get it," Louis said. "I heard he wasn't even poor. That his father's a cardiologist in Atlanta and his mother's got more money that God. He just occasionally mows a lawn now and again for appearances. He's faux poor, Esther. It's just not right."

Esther looked at him calmly, as if studying him for the first time, this trembling husband of hers. Finally, she appeared to come to some conclusion, and she leaned over to Louis, pressed her lips against his forehead, held them there in a dry kiss, pulled away, smiled a forlorn smile that began and faded simultaneously, and then flipped off the television and turned out the lights.

The next week, she began her slow migration to a condo in Atlanta.

• • •

"Perhaps I made the wrong choice," Louis said. "Maybe many wrong choices. Perhaps I am selfish, and this is my punishment by the powers that be. Maybe I deserve to lose Esther."

He and Scooter were smoking cigarettes at the library, which was where they spent their afternoons. During the three years Louis had lived in Blyght, their schedules had somehow melded into one. In the mornings, they worked on their separate projects, at noon they met for lunch at Kimmie's, the afternoons were spent in the library, and when that became too dull, they retired to MK's. Louis's appearance had grown rough, slightly askew, boozy even. His face bristled in white whiskers. His eyes watered. Tiny red veins burst on the sides of his nose. His thinning hair hung limp around his pink scalp.

"Nah," Scooter said. "The fates don't give a shit about you." He punched out his cigarette in the ashtray. "Hell's right here," he said sadly, poking a finger against his pale forehead. He always looked too clean, too well groomed and without a tan for a manual laborer, a label he gave himself often and offhandedly to anyone who wandered near. As in, *I don't know much about much, seeing as how I basically cut grass for a living, but if you ask me,* and so on.

But in spite of himself, Louis was drawn to the young man. Partially because he could not quell his need to know what Scooter was up to, what he was writing, what his editor or agent or publisher had said. But also because he was lonely with Esther gone most of the time, terrified that he still couldn't seem to finish anything, not a story, not a vignette, not a scene. Everything felt false and flat, and to be honest, Scooter was the only one who seemed interested.

"It's your ego," Scooter said. "Your ego is getting in the way of your work and your marriage. Not the fates. Just tell the woman you love her. Get in your car and drive to Atlanta and tell her she's coming home where she belongs whether she likes it or not."

"I don't know," Louis said. "Esther doesn't take well to demands."

Louis wasn't so sure he wanted Esther around all the time, wasn't sure he could endure her disapproving spells of desolate staring and silence. Or even worse, those moments of heaving sighing, her repeated question: What have we done with our lives? He liked the current state of their relationship, the drama of her swooping into town for a weekend of attempted reconciliation, the occasional sex, the frequent arguing, her inevitable leaving. She'd been leaving him for three years now, and he was used to things the way they were.

Later, at MK's, Scooter grabbed his cloth sack, fished around for a moment, and then handed Louis a book with no photo or artwork on the cover, just a black background with *Life in These Parts* written in all white letters. Beneath that, "A Novel by Scott Light."

"Some good news." Scooter shrugged. "For you."

"Black?" Louis said. His heart felt huge, adrift in his chest. He thought he might be sick. This was Scooter's third novel. Three novels published in three years. Louis knew it was coming, but its physicality had a surprising effect on him. He envisioned a hearty, congratulatory laugh, saw his hand reach out to slap his buddy on the shoulder in a gesture of goodwill and celebration, but none of this seemed to be happening.

"Black?" he repeated.

They toasted. They toasted again. They ordered more drinks. Usually, Louis refused to leave MK's until Scooter did, refused to be the old man who couldn't keep up. Sometimes he overcompensated by drinking more than too much, gesticulating wildly. "I'm a bad man," Louis repeated to anyone and everyone throughout the night. "You just don't know."

A woman materialized whom Scooter appeared to know well enough. Since Scooter's literary success, a few of the more cerebral women around town had begun flirting with him, asking him what they thought to be piercing questions about his work, and Scooter attempted to engage them in sexy repartee, although his clumsy gestures and efforts at conversation always came off as more an approximation of nonchalant magnetism than sincere interest. He usually ended up passing the women off to Louis until the end of the evening, when they found their way back to Scooter.

The young woman and Louis danced. She cried about someone else, clumps of black eyeliner gathering in the corners of her eyes. Louis cooed a few things that made her dimple, made her tell him how sweet he was. He put his hand against her wet cheek and held it there, and he tried to feel compassion for the sincerity of her pain but could only thrill in his proximity to it. "I'm a bad man," he told her.

Around midnight, Scooter hung his arm around her waist, sipped the last of his bourbon, and winked at Louis. Louis went home alone.

• • •

The next day when it was time to go to Kimmie's for lunch, Louis didn't stir. He sat in his underwear and black socks on the front porch of his barn-turned-home in Blyght, Georgia, and he didn't stir. When the phone rang, he let it ring. For hours, he read this passage about a character named Hank from *Life in These Parts* over and over again, until the ink began to blur and mutate into something live shifting across the page:

> It wasn't so much as if he were dying. He was already dead. A walking shell. Trying to rediscover who he really is. Who he might be. Most nights he'd get drunk. Tell stories. About better days.
>
> Or worse.

Cry incoherently about a young wife left behind. A son. Forever two. Abandoned. Abandoned for the dream. Him wanting. To become bigger than what he was. To create worlds with words. He did. No one cared. Including himself.

"It was the right thing to do," he'd say to anyone who would listen in Millie's Pub. It was the only thing to do.

He returned inside, showered, shaved, dressed, went to the dining room, and made himself a drink from the bourbon in the antique crystal canister that sat on the antique mahogany bar, both of which Esther had painstakingly chosen to match the décor of the old barn.

When the doorbell rang, he didn't answer it. When it rang again, he knew it would be Scooter, perhaps there to explain why Louis and his life had been caricatured in his superficial novel. Or, knowing Scooter, just there to see why Louis had stood him up for their lunch date, oblivious as always.

"You're not welcome here," Louis said, opening the door.

The young girl standing on his doorstep shoved a jug of wine at him. She had a manuscript tucked under her arm like a baguette.

"But I brought wine," she said. "My thesis adviser told me Pinkie Malone got a blurb from Peter Thorn by driving across country and showing up at his door with a bottle of wine, and so here I am." She smiled, her incisors, the shade of an old bruise, skinny as toothpicks. "Is it working?"

Her name was March Gayle Dewlittle. She was fresh out of graduate school. He vaguely remembered a couple of sweet-scented letters praising his work and lamenting the quality of the graduate workshop from a March Gayle Dewlittle, a young writer who hailed from Ohio but attended graduate school in Florida. The letters Louis received from writing students all sounded alike. When he answered them, if he answered them, he always responded with the same line: "Don't let them stifle your voice." He assumed that the recipients found his reply profound and moving.

When reading March's letters, he'd envisioned a healthy blond midwestern girl, big bones, sturdy, built-in handholds for hips, with breasts that announced themselves as breasts—not the apologetic nubs of the starved blond-bobbed southern girls in Blyght. He'd imagined those large breasts, the way they creased thickly when she bent to write a letter to him, her long hair falling over her unwrinkled brow, her heart so midwestern and sincere that it thumped audibly against her crisp white blouse.

Only March didn't look so sweetly midwestern. She wore the familiar writer uniform. Black, almost feline glasses. No makeup. Colorless, short, spiky, angry hair. She was so skeletal that Louis could count her ribs beneath her black turtleneck, could see the half-moons of her hip bones jutting against her gray wool skirt. There were no breasts.

"You don't look like your pictures on your book jackets," March said skeptically.

"You want to see my driver's license?" Louis said.

HA. HA. March said. HA. HA.

They stared at each other.

"May I come in?" She thrust the jug of wine, one step up from the boxed kind, in his face again. "I brought wine."

"That's a fine grape you have there," Louis said, standing aside so March could enter.

"I'm just out of graduate school. Things are tight." March tried a winning smile with her graveyard of teeth. "Besides, it's the kind June and Fern get drunk on in the murder scene in *Winter Breaks.* I thought you'd appreciate it."

"Of course," Louis said. "How clever. You've read my books."

"Well," March said, "you want to get some glasses or something?"

"Why don't we just drink it straight out of the jug," he said. "That's what Fern and June did. They just drank it right down."

March looked unsure. Louis yanked the jug out of her hands and walked to the living room without inviting her to follow.

"This is a nice place you've got here," March said.

"Esther decorated it," Louis said, plopping down on the couch. An old converted carriage wheel served as a coffee table. "She's a genius with velvet and dried carnations."

"Your wife?" March said, sitting on the matching opposite couch. "Is she here?" She peered about the room as if Louis had shoved Esther into the curio cabinet.

"No," Louis said, patting the spot next to him. "She left me." He unscrewed the bottle of wine, flashed March a smile. "You know women." He patted the spot next to him again. "Sit here so we can talk."

March slid onto the couch, pressed herself into the armrest as far away from Louis as possible.

"She used to write short stories. But now she finds them tedious, finds all fiction dishonest somehow, predatory even."

"Your wife hates fiction?" March's face looked almost attractive in its confusion, the bit of flesh on her brow drawn together in an indentation. Louis put his finger right there, just at that crease of flesh.

"A crease indeed!" he said. "You've delivered."

"Pardon?" March smiled nervously. Louis dropped his finger, let it brush against the bridge of her nose.

"She was a student of mine. That's how we met. She was very young and very, very sexy. Her writing stank. Go figure."

"How sweet," March said, taking a pull from the jug of wine. When she smiled, her teeth were stained a darker shade of purple.

"A bruise blooming," Louis said.

"What?"

"Did I say something?" Louis said, taking the jug from March. He drank for some time, then handed it back to her. "Not so sweet. I was married to my high school sweetheart at the time. I had a son. Esther and I had an affair. We had sex in my office."

"Things happen," March said. She looked concerned. Very concerned. She took off her glasses. She rubbed at her brown eyes, gauzy with moisture. "It must have been really hard on you. Writers feel things so deeply. I know I do." March paused for a moment. She felt. "I hurt someone who loved me once," she said. "I had to. It's what my work needed. Sometimes you have to make sacrifices like that for your work." She put her hand on Louis's.

"You think?" Louis said. He put his other hand on top of hers. "A hand sandwich," he said. "Yummy." He bent down, bit the tip of her finger, hard.

March yelped, yanked back her hand.

Louis laughed. "Don't you remember?" he said. "That's from *A Pilgrimage in Georgia.*"

"Oh," March said. She recovered her smile. "Of course. Of course it is." Then, "Wow. It just hit me. I mean, like just now. I'm sitting on a fucking couch with Louis Peter and we're talking about his work."

"Well, let's have it," Louis said.

"Have what?" March said.

"The manuscript," Louis said.

"Oh." March handed him her book, titled *A Mississippi Night Dark.* Louis read the opening line aloud: "The graying dew fell thick like honey or night or promise on the yielding, soft, sweet skin of Milah Jo, the last refrains of the night's call a-rubbin' weary legs together, and in her nakedness, in her want, Milah Jo knew the calling of the Lord and Billy Jenkins was in her belly, soon to be in her arms and at the achin' of her breast, and she would call it love, she would call him Son."

Louis paused and then said, "I thought you were from Ohio."

"I am," March said, "but who wants to write about Ohio?" She explained that she'd been to Mississippi when her family stopped to see a great-aunt on the way to Disney World one year, and she'd been touched by . . . something, she couldn't name it, and felt a kinship with the alienation of the gothic South.

"Sherwood Anderson," Louis said.

"Who?"

"Sherwood Anderson wrote about Ohio," Louis said. "Never mind. This is fine work. Something else." For a moment, he felt a pang of guilt, not because he'd lied, but because the lie came so easily.

"Really?"

"Oh yeah," Louis said.

"It comes out in the fall," March said, sipping nervously from the wine jug. "I thought you might take a look at it and then give it a blurb, but only if you respect it, only if the work stands on its own."

For a moment they sat in silence, Louis drinking the wine without offering any to March. He remembered the day his first manuscript was accepted for publication. Anything could have happened, and it had, just none of the things Louis had wanted.

"A toast to your new literary success," Louis said finally, taking a pull off the jug then handing it back to March, who did the same.

"We should do something special to commemorate this moment," Louis announced. "Something *deeply literary.*"

"You think?" March said.

"Of course."

When Louis stuffed a drunk March into his Volvo, he had no idea where he wanted to take her, only that he didn't want to be in that godforsaken *Bonanza* set for another moment. He needed to *move.* He needed to *go.* He had too much jittery energy; his legs vibrated against the leather car seat.

So when March asked where they were going, Louis told her it was a surprise. It was only when he saw a mile marker sign to Milledgeville that he thought up the idea of getting drunk at Flannery O'Connor's grave. But Milledgeville was more than an hour away, and Louis felt a little too woozy to be driving that far. So when he saw the exit to Wesley, he took it, following the signs to the historic district that he knew every small southern town had. He picked a house with white latticework and a huge front porch and parked the car under the sweep of a magnolia tree.

"Where are we going?" March asked for the tenth time. "Tell me."

"We're here," Louis said.

"Where's here?" March was starting to look suspicious. She pulled her legs off the dashboard where she'd thrown them in carefree spirits just minutes before.

"This is the home where Flannery O'Connor drew her last breath."

"You're kidding," March said, twisting in her seat to get a better look at the house in the fading light. "Here? But there's no plaque or anything. And anyway, I thought she lived in Milledgeville."

"They don't have a plaque up so crazy people like us don't hang out here." He grinned a conspirator's grin.

"Neat," March said. "I have to take a piss."

She got out of the car. Louis didn't even pretend not to watch as March lifted her skirt, wrenched her tights down around her knees, and squatted, her skin, so pasty at Louis's home, transformed by the moonlight, exquisitely pale and fragile, like nothing hands should touch.

When she slid back into the Volvo, she seemed less drunk and more resolved.

"If we're going to do it," she said, "let's do it. I have a plane to catch in the morning."

Without a word, he reached for her, slid his hands over her spindly body, and forgot himself, knowing nothing but the warmth of March Dewlittle.

And of course he wrote the blurb for her first novel.

• • •

Months later, when he threw the complimentary copy her publicist sent him on the bar at MK's to show Scooter—whom he'd already forgiven over a bottle of bourbon and mutual confessions of various insecurities—Scooter became incensed by the praise March had received from the literary community, by the awards for which she'd been nominated.

"The lovechild of O'Connor and Faulkner? What were these idiots thinking?" Scooter said. "Why in the world did you put your name on this shit?" He pitched the book on the floor. A dolled-up country girl sat next to him, a girl Louis had seen Scooter's arm around a few times lately, and she calmly lit a cigarette, took a sip of her drink.

Louis smiled. "Sometimes you got to pay the piper," he said, and felt silly saying it.

They toasted, and the girl raised her own glass with them. And they talked. And while they talked, Louis watched the girl, a beer in one hand, a cigarette in the other. Her laughter was careless and loose.

Scooter winked at the girl, and she smiled back shyly, her eyes brilliant with artless want.

Louis thought: If I asked her, really asked her, would Esther line her eyes in electric blue? Would she agree to park under the streetlamp behind the Pig? Would she drink Milwaukee's Best?

If anything, he'd be content just to see her waiting for him on the porch when he arrived home. And maybe this evening things would be different. Maybe this time she would understand the joy of unstudied, uncontaminated passion. "Close your eyes," she might say. "Please," she might say.

Then the lights flipped on, and the bartender yelled the familiar *You don't have to go home; but you can't stay here.* Bottles clinked sharply against bottles in the trash cans; stunned patients shuffled out into the night. Scooter eased his arm around the curve of the girl's neck, the starkness of its pale skin somehow sobering, and she suddenly seemed to Louis just a girl, not a thing of wonder or possibility.

witnessing

The house sits at the end of a cul-de-sac, the last of a chain of McMansions modeled after Mediterranean villas. The yard is treeless, the live oaks Rose remembers covering this area in her childhood cleared to facilitate rapid construction. Bared to the morning sun, the pink stucco house looks sunburned. If Rose had the money, she would have done things differently, something she thinks about often. Left the trees. Built a little hedge of azaleas. Maybe even a gazebo in the front yard. Nothing too flashy, just a nice, shady place to kick back on a warm summer afternoon.

Before Rose can ring the bell, the door opens. Cecilia stands in the doorway in a long silk nightgown and a scarlet wig styled in a pageboy.

"You're here," she says. "That's good." A heart-shaped birthmark sinks into the crease of her smile. Rose has never seen Cecilia close up in person. She didn't expect her to be so striking.

Cecilia turns her back to Rose and begins walking through the vaulted foyer. "We'll talk in my bedroom so I can lie down," she says over her shoulder. "I assume you know where it is."

In fact, Rose has been inside the house only once. Cecilia was in the hospital at the time, and Baxter responded, as he usually does when Cecilia suffers a setback, by getting radiantly soused at dinner. Rose had to drive him home and help him into bed, where they'd made love gravely. After he passed out, she'd wandered around the silent house, studying the photos of Baxter and Cecilia in Paris, Rome, Bangkok, reading the little notes they scattered around the house for each other. (You are the soul of my world. I love you like piña coladas on the beach at sunset. Remember the corn maize in Kansas?) Overwhelmed, Rose hid in the master bedroom for almost an hour, rummaging through drawers, looking for something—pimple cream, yeast infection medicine—anything to make Cecilia seem base and ordinary, because strangely, the sicker Cecilia gets, the more ethereal she becomes to Baxter.

"Come here." Cecilia pats the velvet bedspread as she sits. "If you stand, it would only be polite for me to stand, and to be frank, I don't think I'm able."

Rose sits on the bed; the bells on her Christmas sweater jingle stupidly. Cecilia's flank is so close that the heat is perceptible. She smells of lavender and vanilla. Rose discreetly sniffs her own wrist: dishwashing detergent and fingernail polish remover.

"I thought you'd be blonder," Cecilia says. She moves as if she's going to touch Rose's hair, then seems to reconsider, her hand lingering in midair. "From what Baxter said about you, I mean. Although your shade is quite nice."

"Why am I here?" Rose blurts out. When Cecilia had called the night before and asked Rose to come over, Rose had been too shocked to question her, too nervous to mumble anything other than yes. She'd assumed that Cecilia wanted to ask about the affair, but after thinking about it, she couldn't imagine that there was anything that Baxter wouldn't tell his wife himself.

"I don't know," Cecilia says. "Why are you here? Why are any of us here, that's the real question, huh?" She tosses her skeletal arms into the air and tilts her head back as if addressing the gods. Then she stares at Rose, deadly serious, waiting for an answer. Tiny red veins pop against the white of her eyeballs; her pupils are dilated, so large that Rose feels she could dive into them. Cecilia is extraordinarily high.

"You asked me to come," Rose says. "I thought you might have something important to tell me. Something about Baxter." Three weeks ago, he'd sent flowers to Rose's work with a note about how special her heart was and how she'd go far in the world. She hasn't heard from him since.

"I did, didn't I?" Cecilia says softly. She stares out the bay window. Two neighborhood girls, out of school for Christmas break, are poking something with a stick in the drainage ditch. There is not a cloud in the sky. "It's a beautiful day," she says finally. "Too hot for December, but beautiful all the same. When Baxter and I were first married, he surprised me with a snow machine at Christmas. He set it up right at the front door so some would blow in the living room. My family's been down here forever. I'd never seen more than a powdering of snow." She turns to Rose. "That was a nice thing for him to do, I suppose, although I had to clean up the carpet."

"I hate cold," Rose says. "It's, well, it's cold."

Cecilia laughs as if this is the funniest thing she's ever heard. She slaps Rose's thigh, then wags her finger as though Rose is a mischievous girl who just tried to outsmart an adult; and suddenly, Rose is tired. She couldn't sleep after Cecilia's phone call last night. And she's running late. Today's her company Christmas party. A Toyota dealership, where Rose processes orders for parts. ("And what do you do?" men ask her at bars on the occasional nights she goes out, looking for something better. "Parts," she says, trying to sound cryptically funny and sexy, "I do parts.")

"Well, you know I approve of you tremendously," Cecilia says. "I'm grateful Baxter has had someone to talk to through all of this. It's been quite the ordeal."

"Baxter said you didn't mind," Rose says. She studies her tennis shoes, which she'd decorated in sequined Christmas trees. It had seemed clever at the time, an idea she got out of some ladies' magazine, but now the misshapen trees horrify her. "I didn't believe him at first."

Baxter admitted that Cecilia found out about the affair, although he wouldn't mention how, last Christmas. They were supposed to exchange gifts that evening, toast to the end of the year, the beginning of the new. Instead, they sat on opposite ends of the sofa and opened their gifts guiltily. Something had shifted. Rose felt strange about Cecilia knowing, as if she and Baxter had been set up by a doting aunt. When Baxter began offering little tidbits of advice from Cecilia—how maybe Rose should go back to school for her bachelor's or how she shouldn't let her mother ride her so hard—Rose told him she wasn't a pet project and threatened to leave him. But by then it was too late. She already loved him in that mysterious way most love—not quite able to explain the why.

"It's all very French, don't you think?" Cecilia grins. "My people are Scotch-Irish, but maybe I have a Parisian soul. I've been told that before, you know."

"I'm a Danish," Rose says, then realizes that she's just announced she's a pastry.

"Enough of Baxter," Cecilia says with a sweep of her arm. She lays herself lengthwise on the bed, a mound of satin-covered pillows supporting her, the bottoms of her feet pressed firmly against Rose's thigh. She wiggles her toes, the nails painted bright blue, the color a teenager would choose. "I'm sure two intelligent women can find something more interesting to talk about than a man. This is the age of feminism, you know." She laughs. Balls her hand and punches the air. "Girrrrrrl power. Or whatever nonsense the kids say these days."

"I need to go," Rose says. She points to the dancing elves on her sweater. "It's the company Christmas party—"

"How old are you?" Cecilia says. "Twenty-nine, thirty?"

"Thirty-two." It sounds strange, the number. Rose sometimes forgets how old she is. She can still remember the junior college boys who hung around her high school some afternoons, asking her age, and her teasing voice when she responded: Sixteen. That was half a lifetime ago, and if pressed, Rose is not sure if she could account for most of it.

"Well, that's young," Cecilia says. "You don't think it is now, but you will. I'm fifty-six. When you're young, you never think you'll be fifty, then one day you just are. Which is fine.

But this you never expect." She reaches under her pillow, pulls out what looks like a fanny pack, and throws it onto Rose's lap. "My friendly travel-size chemo. Goes anywhere you go. When it comes to this, you start thinking and doing things you never considered. Desperate things. But, then again, I'm sure you never thought you'd be single in your thirties and having an affair with a married man. Do you understand what I'm saying?"

"Sweet Cecilia," Baxter had said that first night he and Rose had met at happy hour at a local bar. Over martinis he'd explained his wife's sickness, the deterioration of her body and their sex life. He wore a navy tie with different-colored golfing tees, his graying hair thick and slicked over his crown. He was neither handsome nor unattractive. Love at first sight, Rose would tell him later, because he liked hearing such things.

What she fell for was his love story with Cecilia. It seems pathetic now. But in the moment she had finally felt important, as though her existence were essential to something bigger and it no longer mattered that she'd never finished her nursing degree, or that she hadn't lost the fifteen pounds she's been meaning to lose for years now, or that she was over thirty and didn't have a husband to send off to work or kids to pack school lunches for, because Baxter had told her he needed her, and she'd believed him.

They had sex in the alley behind the bar. Afterward, Baxter said, "Thank you," very politely. It took Rose only the three hours they spent in the bar to convince herself that their affair was acceptable.

"I've been reading about alternatives lately." Cecilia kicks the fanny pack of chemo in Rose's lap to get her attention. "Alternatives to this."

"I'm so sorry," Rose says. "I know it must be—"

"Enough of the pity party," Cecilia snaps. She opens the bedside drawer, which is filled with prescription bottles and syringes, the only messy space in the fastidiously neat room, and produces a crumpled business card and hands it to Rose. On the corner, there are two hands folded in prayer sprouting little angel wings.

"A contact reflex analyst and psychic. He reads the body's energy fields and reflexes. Very powerful people spend great amounts of money for his time." Cecilia takes the card from Rose and cups it solemnly in her hand. "And he's agreed to see me. He's agreed to see me today."

"I have to go," Rose repeats, but already she feels as if any control she had over the situation is slipping. Outside, neighborhood girls shriek at each other; one has what the other one wants.

"Limited," Cecilia says. "If I had to think of a word to describe Baxter, that's the one. Can't think outside of the B-O-X." She draws an imaginary box in the air with her index finger. "Don't get me wrong. He's a good man. Just limited in his reach."

"Perhaps," Rose whispers, feeling slightly disloyal.

"So you'll help me?" Cecilia says. Color rises high in her cheeks. Her hands jerk in little twitches. Rose cannot tell if she is excited or angry.

"Baxter refuses to take me. He insists I'm trying to kill myself with such nonsense. I can't drive anymore because of the seizures, and I would prefer that no one find out. Besides, it would give us a chance to get to know each other." She looks at Rose, hard. "Don't you think we should know each other?"

Rose thinks of the last time she saw Baxter. He had mentioned the week before that Cecilia was a drama major in college when they met, how he went to drama club parties just to get a glimpse of her. He'd spoken about her so wistfully that Rose spent the next two days reading from her high school Shakespeare text in front of the mirror. *How should I your true love know from another one? By his cockle hat and staff, And his sandal shoon.* She'd read for him on their next date, but the lines had sounded funny in her country accent, even worse when she'd tried to hide it, and she didn't know what half of it meant. He'd stared at her blankly for an embarrassingly long moment, then made an excuse about forgetting something that he needed to take care of and left.

"And let's be honest, dear," Cecilia says when Rose doesn't answer. "It's the least you could do, considering."

● ● ●

Cecilia stares out the window of Rose's Toyota, laconic and distant. They are half an hour outside of Montgomery, Cecilia's Gucci bag pitching across the backseat. Cecilia has changed into a navy silk pants suit, the tufts of her cream blouse blossoming at her neck, her lips subdued in frosty pink lipstick. Her outfit costs more than Rose makes in a month.

Rose took the meandering back roads because Cecilia insisted they experience the scenery. If this was to be her last road trip, she wanted to see something besides nondescript highway with exits to cookie-cutter strip malls. Near the Georgia border,

Cecilia cracks her window and makes a game of counting the number of double-wides wrapped in icicle-shaped Christmas lights.

"They're not kidding around with this Christmas stuff, are they," she says. "It's like a ludicrous competition in redneckness. God knows the amount of money they spend."

Rose thinks of the small trailer she lives in, how she spent an entire weekend outlining it in Christmas lights and rigging a life-size illuminated Frosty that teetered on the stamp-size patch of grass she calls her front yard. And then Baxter sent the note and the flowers, and she got drunker than drunk and ripped it all down, figuring why bother?

They hit another tiny town, one of a dozen along the way, as identical in their poverty as strip malls: red-brick false-front buildings, rotted, defunct gas stations, graffitied video stores, the doors long since closed—the carrion left behind when the Wal-Marts and the Applebee's moved close to town and the mills left for Mexico.

At a stoplight, they pull up alongside a blond teenage girl with a nose ring the size of a washer shoving Hardees' hash browns into her mouth. Her souped-up Honda Prelude—gleaming silver rims, a yellow fireball blazing down the side—palpitates with rap music: *Everywhere I look, everywhere I go, I see the same ho. Don't get mad. I'm only being real.*

Cecilia leans over Rose, scrutinizes the girl, then shakes her head, her wig slipping to one side. "What's with country girls these days?" she says, her breath sour on Rose's cheek. "They all want to be ghetto whores." She mouths to the girl: "What's your problem? You should be in school."

The girl flashes a bellicose smile, flips them the finger, then allows her mouth to gape open, a plug of half-chewed potatoes bouncing on her darting tongue.

"You're going to get us shot," Rose says, shoving Cecilia back into her seat. "You can't do that kind of shit out here." She looks back at the girl, shrugs apologetically, twirls her finger at her temple to indicate that Cecilia is nuts, which she decides is true enough. But the girl's fumbling with her CD player; she doesn't even see Rose.

"The world's going to hell in a handbasket," Cecilia says. She flexes her hands the way a man does when considering a fight. "But that's the beauty of dying. You can let everyone know just that, and what's the worst thing that could happen? Huh? Shoot me? Stab me? Well, bring it on, I say. Do me the favor."

Without a pause, Cecilia calmly opens the passenger door and vomits neatly onto the street. Then she fishes in her handbag, takes out several bottles of pills, pours a wad into her hand, and swallows them dry.

"Drive," she says, pointing to the light to indicate that it's turned green.

• • •

The address on the business card is for a mom-and-pop motel attached to a liquor store on the outskirts of Macon. Behind the motel is a small trailer, presumably the owner's, with dead ferns hanging from the porch overhang.

"Hand me that card," Rose says. "We must have read it wrong."

"This is the place," Cecilia says softly, and Rose can hear

genuine fear in her voice. "Mr. Meekle owns the motel. We're supposed to get a room, and he'll meet us there at two."

A mangy, plucked-looking cat leaps onto the hood of the car, stretches languidly, then plops into a curl.

Cecilia lifts her wig as if tipping a hat. Tufts of gray hair lurch from her scalp in clumps like Spanish moss. "We must have the same stylist," she says. Her eyes dare Rose to show pity.

"I think you look great," Rose says, because she does. Even ill, Cecilia is one of the best-looking women her age that Rose has ever seen.

What Rose doesn't say: No master healer frequented by wealthy, satisfied clients would live in such a hovel.

The front-desk clerk, a fleshy woman in a Christmas sweater identical to Rose's, watches a soap opera from a lazy chair wedged behind the counter. Behind her is a cross-stitched sign: GOD IS HERE.

On the TV, a couple struggles in an agitated embrace. The clerk is entranced; even after Cecilia rings the service bell twice, the woman doesn't budge until a commercial flickers onto the screen.

"Nice sweater," the woman says to Rose. "You got the earrings, too. I told my daughter I should get the earrings, but she said to wait for the after Thanksgiving sales, and when I went back, they were gone. Ain't that always the way of it? Y'all got a credit card? I'll need to run it in case you make long-distance calls or use the pay-per-view."

The clerk moves slowly, as if underwater, and it takes her a full minute to walk to the other side of the counter to run Cecilia's credit card. When she shuffles back, she hands the card to

Cecilia, looks her up and down, then pats her tenderly on the hand. "Don't you worry. You've come to a holy place."

"Praise Jesus," Cecilia says flatly.

Their hotel room is clean, but that's all that can be said for it. A tiny card table in the corner, two mismatched chairs, a double bed in a faded floral spread, a wooden veneer dresser with an old TV, a shag carpet the rusty red of dried blood. It smells of cheap air freshener and cigarettes.

Cecilia immediately whips out Lysol from her bag, begins spraying down the bed, the table, the bathroom. She yanks off the bedspread, folds it neatly, and shoves it on a chair. Then she picks up the TV remote between her thumb and index finger and drops it into the wastebasket. "The dirtiest thing in the room," she says, pumping her tongue against her cheek, the same gesture the car salesmen at the dealership use to indicate that a fuckable woman is on the lot. "Men hold it and God knows what else while they're watching their nasty movies."

This is not the Cecilia that Baxter described on the many nights he wept over her: the woman who could make a stunning centerpiece out of tree twigs and pinecones, the woman who could speak three languages fluently, the woman who once fired the gardener for urinating on the back lawn.

Cecilia heads to the bathroom sink, begins splashing water onto her face. "What did you think of that receptionist nut?" she yells over the water. "This is a *holy* place. Has she been inside one of these rooms?" When she emerges from the bathroom, her lips are coated in fresh pink lipstick, her cheeks smeared with too much rouge. "I need a drink," she announces, and before Rose can mention that maybe a drink is not such a good idea, Cecilia is out the door.

Rose thinks of turning on the TV, but she's too lazy to walk to the trash can to get the remote. Instead, she lies back on the bed, thinking she should call her boss to tell him she is missing work, which should be obvious by now. Kids have written on the ceiling. Apparently, Johnny B. wuz here, Connie luvs Eric, and April L. sux big dick!!!, which Rose thinks is supposed to be a compliment. She's half-asleep when Cecilia returns, a bottle of wine under each arm.

"You need a cup?" she says. "Or do you just drink it straight from the bottle?" Before Rose can react, Cecilia pulls a fancy corkscrew from her suit pocket, which she must have brought from home for just this occasion, whips the cork from the bottle in record speed, and fills two flimsy hotel cups.

"Maybe you shouldn't be drinking on all that medication," Rose says.

"Probably not," Cecilia says. She finishes the wine in a long swallow, pours herself another.

Rose picks up the phone book from the bedside table, flips the pages nervously, then puts it back down. There's a photo of an expensive sailboat on the cover, which doesn't make much sense. The ocean is hours away.

"Do you sail?" Cecilia asks. "Baxter loves it. I mainly drink martinis and suntan, which I guess I could do anywhere, but a sailboat works, too. The sea makes you feel small. In a good way."

"My sailboat's in the shop," Rose says, and instead of taking offense, Cecilia lifts her glass to Rose.

"Touché. I can see why Baxter enjoys your company. I bet you keep him on his toes."

"I don't think this is a good idea," Rose says. "I mean, I don't think I want to be here."

"Then pretend," Cecilia says. She walks to the window and pulls up the shades, the brilliant midday sun garish.

"There's a squirrel that plays outside my window at home," Cecilia says. "I've decided he's male because of the way he holds his tail, fluffed out and stiff. Sometimes I talk to him, about any little thing. Something I read in the paper. A funny joke I heard. For the most part he's been good company. He keeps his mouth shut."

"Maybe you should take a nap," Rose says. Cecilia is leaning heavily against the window frame, and if she passes out, Rose isn't sure she could get her on the bed. "Why don't you drink some water?"

"The other day he finally talked back," Cecilia says. "You know what he said? He said, 'I'll be here long after you're gone, and I'm just a fucking squirrel.' I told him that wasn't a nice thing to say."

"You're drunk," Rose says, which is starting to sound like a good idea.

"Believe me," Cecilia says, "I need to get a lot drunker."

Outside, the parking lot is completely empty, not a car in sight. A billboard in neon green advertises THE BUNNY HOLE, a gentleman's club.

"Who knew such a place existed," Cecilia says, allowing the shades to fall.

• • •

Rose is awakened by a soft rapping, and by the time she opens her eyes and sits up, Cecilia is wobbling at the door beside a wizened man wearing blue-jean overalls and a Braves cap. His face is blank and stoic, a look Rose associates with country farmers who have plenty of land and little money. He seems to be close to a hundred.

"You the one?" he says to Cecilia, who nods yes, closing the door behind him.

He tips his cap and offers his hand, palm up. In spite of his age, his hand is steady. "Might as well get the unpleasant part over and done with." Cecilia snatches her handbag off the bed, fumbles with her wallet, then places a stack of bills in his hand. He shoves the bills into the front pocket of his overalls.

In comparison with the front-desk clerk, Mr. Meekle is absolutely agile. He glides straight to the closet and hauls out a small wooden platform, which he places in front of the dresser.

He looks at Rose, says, "You can stay, but not a peep out of you. I need absolute quiet to connect." He rolls up the sleeves to his flannel shirt, revealing arms covered in purplish bruises and cuts, the ancient, scabrous arms of the old. Immediately, the mood in the room is somber.

"So your body rebels against you," Mr. Meekle says to Cecilia.

"Yes," Cecilia sighs.

"Did you bring your current medication?"

Cecilia nods, then pulls seven or so bottles from her purse, lines them up neatly on the dresser, and steps unevenly onto the crude wooden platform.

Mr. Meekle tells her to relax, then allows his hands to tremble over her body like a divining rod, never touching, just humming across skin. They stop on her belly.

"Here," he says.

"Yes."

He lingers there for a long time, his hands pulsating in odd, tiny jerks, then moves down her legs, then back up, past her belly, stopping over the crown of her skull, Cecilia's body careening to and fro from booze or the power of his hands.

"And here," he says.

"Yes," Cecilia whispers. "There, too."

Mr. Meekle grabs one of Cecilia's prescription bottles, places it in her right hand, and tells her he's going to test her. He lifts her left arm until it extends straight from her body as if she were about to salute. "How much Neurontin does this body need?" he asks aloud. This is so the body can hear, he explains. He tugs her arm in a short, curt movement, her entire frame caving in toward him as he counts each pull—"one, two, three"—until her arm hangs at her side. "That means take three of these," he says, taking the bottle from her and replacing it with another.

The whole process takes almost two hours. Both Mr. Meekle and Cecilia hang limp at the end, as if they've endured a bout of lovemaking. Sweat pours down his face, drops catching on the tip of his hawkish nose. Cecilia is wide-eyed and silent, her beauty stark.

Rose watches all of this from her perch on the bed, fascinated and embarrassed at the same time. She's never been witness to such peculiar despair.

"Is there hope?" Cecilia asks.

Mr. Meekle plucks a handkerchief from his pocket, dabs at his forehead, then proceeds to tell Cecilia a tale about a local woman a few years back, a savagely sick woman with months of dying ahead of her, who had the good sense to know when to throw in the towel. She gathered her family around her, said her good-byes, then prayed herself straight to heaven on her own terms. The onlookers claimed to see her spirit gather itself above her, leaving the terrible failing body, and ascending up, up, up. Rose envisions a woman lying in her bed, her family grieving and praying around her, then *swoosh,* the shadow of her flies into the heavens, waving the whole way as if from a pageant float.

"She took control of the situation," he says. "Sometimes release is the only healing left. Do you understand what I'm saying?" He pulls a Ziploc bag filled with dark green leaves from his pocket, slaps it on the dresser, cautions her of its potency, its danger, then tells her to make a tea out of it for pain. Then he's gone.

"Quack," Cecilia says when Mr. Meekle leaves, but Rose can tell that she's deeply shaken. "Ascension and release. I didn't need to pay someone to tell me how to die. Everyone figures that out." Her eyes are strangely bright, almost iridescent. She picks up the bag of medicine Mr. Meekle left, turns it over in her palm, then throws it back on the dresser.

She walks to the table, pours herself a glass of wine. "Just think," she says, "if we were friends, and on our last trip together, this would be cocktail hour, and we would be sipping drinks, coddling our nostalgia, but happy."

"It's that late? My boss is going to kill me." This is Rose's fifth job in three years, and she doesn't need to lose it, but she can't seem to muster the concern to care. It's not like she's a doctor or a teacher, where her presence or absence matters. She processes parts, and if she's fired, there will be another girl working tomorrow who can do the job just as well.

"Forget the dealership," Cecilia says as if reading Rose's mind. "You can do better."

"I'm planning on it," Rose says. "I just need to save a bit more for school. Besides, my job's not so bad. I've had worse."

Cecilia considers this for a moment, sucking on the soft petal of her bottom lip. "Did you ever hear of the story," she says, "about the Persian servant who stumbled upon Death, who threatened him? He begged his master for the fastest horse so he could make it to Tehran by nightfall. Later that day, the master met Death, and he asked why Death had threatened his servant. 'I did not threaten him,' Death said. 'I only showed surprise in still finding him here when I planned to meet him tonight in Tehran.' It's about avoiding death or fate, but I think it can be about avoiding life as well."

"What's that supposed to mean?" Rose says. And suddenly, she's angry. Aside from falling in love with the wrong man, what had she done to piss off God so royally?

"I'm *hungry,*" Cecilia says, her mood shifting from bleak to chipper so fast, Rose wonders if she should fear for her own safety. "I'm never hungry. Do you think there's anything to eat around here?"

Rose gives Cecilia a half-eaten bag of Cheetos she has in her purse, and Cecilia begins shoving them in her mouth like a girl at a slumber party, crumbs spilling down her bodice. "These are delicious," she says. "I haven't had food like this in ages."

Cecilia climbs onto the bed next to Rose, leans back on the

overstuffed pillow, intermittently stuffing Cheetos in her mouth and taking long swigs of wine. Sanguine rivulets dribble down her chin. She doesn't bother to wipe them away.

"We can go now," Rose says. "Baxter must be home. He'll be worried. We could make it back by ten if we take the highway. At least we should call." Rose wondered what she would say. *I have your wife.*

"I saw you that night," Cecilia says, her mouth full of Cheetos. Rose's heart drops to her stomach. "The night Baxter dumped you. I saw you outside my window."

It happened only once. Rose just wanted to understand why, to see what was so special about Cecilia that made Baxter choose her when he was never asked to make the choice.

She'd parked a mile away so no one would see her car and walked, tripping through yards and ditches. Orange lights from suburban homes spilled onto dead grass; silhouettes of wives in kitchens preparing dinners slurred past Rose like a flip book. She'd huddled under Cecilia's bay window, her knees scraping against the stucco house, and watched as Cecilia stood emotionless in front of her full-length mirror in the same nightgown she'd worn this morning. A smiling Baxter walked into the room, passing the window to reach Cecilia, so close that Rose could have touched him if not for the glass. It was very much like an elegant movie with the sound turned off.

At the time, Rose understood that something terrible had gone wrong in her life to bring her to this moment, but she wasn't yet willing to name it. If she did—name it—she would have to give Baxter up. And if she gave Baxter up, what would she have?

"No one should feel that alone," Cecilia says. She smoothes Rose's bangs out of her eyes with her finger. "That's one of the reasons I brought you here. I wanted you to know that I think that. And I wanted to make peace with things. So know that I forgive you."

"No," Rose says. "You don't."

"You're right." Cecilia's hand is hot on Rose's cheek. "I don't. But it has nothing to do with Baxter."

Outside, the winter sun is setting; it filters through the blinds in long honeyed beams.

"I didn't use to be this way," Cecilia says. "It's hard to remember anymore, but surely I was different. That makes it better, thinking of the me before as separate from the me now."

Cecilia crunches the empty Cheetos bag into a ball, pitches it at the trash can, and misses. "I'm hot," she announces, struggling to sit up. "I'm always hot. It's either the medication or menopause, but either way, it's killing me."

Cecilia tries to extricate her arms from her suit coat, but the sleeve catches on her elbow. When Rose tries to help, she brushes her away. Cecilia fumbles with the buttons of her blouse, smearing orange Cheetos seasoning on the cream silk. Finally, she sits half-naked on the bed. Empty skin puddles below her elbows. Her breasts are small and flaccid in her beige bra. And because she is healthy and young but aware that this will not always be the case, Rose cannot help but stare, cannot help but think, *So this is what we all become.*

"I'm going to die," Cecilia says.

"We all are," Rose says.

"Maybe today. Maybe I'm going to die today."

"I don't think it will be today."

"Perhaps I want it to be today. Today is as good a day as any."

Without warning, Rose finds herself crying. She thinks that maybe Cecilia's story about avoiding Death or fate makes sense. Maybe we are all avoiding the lives we're living while we wait for our real lives to begin.

Cecilia slides her hand, all bones, into Rose's. They rest like this for a while, their feet grazing in awkward intimacy.

"Rose," Cecilia says finally, "what's your greatest fear?"

"Is this one of those games?" Rose is reminded of lazy afternoons with her girlfriends when they sprawled out on her Strawberry Shortcake quilt and took quizzes that would reveal what their inner animal was or which celebrity they would date if they lived in the same world as the beautiful people on the slick pages of the magazines. At the time, she didn't understand that these are the moments that linger, the moments that create a past. "Like I tell you what I would name a horse, and you dissect my psyche?"

"Mine's that maybe I'm right," Cecilia says softly, "that maybe there is nothing else other than this."

"We should go home," Rose says, but neither of them moves to leave. When twilight shrouds the room and Rose can no longer see the particulars of Cecilia's face, can no longer be sure if she hears her breath or the soft sighs of the hotel heater, she reaches for Cecilia's chest and feels the faint thump of her unfortunate heart.

"I'm still here," Cecilia whispers. For now, this is enough.

detritus

The day our father left us for good to pursue his dream of becoming a professional bass fisherman, it snowed ten inches in Edna, Alabama. We thought the world was ending or a new one beginning. I had never seen snow before. I was thirteen.

That morning, our mother lay beneath an old mulberry tree in the backyard wearing nothing but a nightgown and slippers, until the leafing arms of the tree, which just the day before had swirled in the gusty spring breeze as if writhing in prayer, grew weighted with snow and drooped toward earth in a humbled slouch, the tips grazing our mother's slippered feet.

"It's a sign," our mother said.

"Nimbostratus, Noah," Lucie said to me. She peered at our mother through the frosted kitchen window. "That's what them clouds are called. Nimbostratus."

For an eleven-year-old, everyone considered Lucie freakishly smart, which made what Molly was an even greater tragedy, although at the time she was simply our sister who did not speak.

None of us owned real winter clothing. So we improvised. Lucie squeezed on several pairs of her Sunday tights under a bunny jumpsuit our mother had bought her the previous Easter. I made a scarf out of a table runner. We raided our father's drawers and pilfered his wool socks to use as mittens, figuring he wouldn't need them in the balmy paradise of southern Florida, where he said the bass grew fat and sleek as seals. We wrapped Molly, a little lump of a toddler, in the heaviest bedspread we could find, then hurled ourselves out the front door and into an alien landscape. The snow: magical against our faces.

Lucie propped Molly against the cragged trunk of the mulberry tree, then we pranced like nymphs, singing "Frosty the Snowman" until the words didn't sound like words anymore. Our mother remained perfectly still, her palms lifted toward the snow-heavy sky in supplication.

Around noon, Pete Fundak skidded over on snowshoes fashioned from pot lids and rope. "What's up with your mom?" he said, wiping frozen mucus from his thin mustache. Pete was only fifteen, but he somehow looked like a grown man, and the senior girls at school *ahhhed* over his sulky, pained, I-come-from-a-fucked-up-home glower. I was barely taller than Lucie and wouldn't see the dark facial fuzz of full-blown puberty for another couple of years. Pete and I had been best friends since he blew up a frog in my mailbox in first grade. I worked hard not to be envious.

"A sign," Lucie said from the middle of her cartwheel, her pink bunny ears dipped in snow.

"Oh," Pete said, not surprised, because our mother saw many signs in the world, although usually on a much smaller scale: A dancing tomato in a TV commercial meant Jesus wanted us to eat our vegetables; an eyelash in an eye meant that Jesus wanted Lucie to sit still long enough to have her bangs trimmed on the back porch before she went blind. Pete had a father he'd never met and a mother who weighed four hundred pounds. He wasn't one to point fingers.

"Want to go sliding down the gully?" he asked, and we left Molly under the tree and my mother staring into sky and Lucie spinning in the snow and passed the morning slipping down the gully behind Pete's house on soggy cardboard boxes.

When our fingers and toes grew too numb to grasp the roots twined across the banks of the gully to heft ourselves over the lip of the ledge, we went to Pete's house for lunch. His mother made pickle-and-mustard sandwiches, moving from fridge to counter in a lurching blur while seated in an armless office chair Pete had rigged with training wheels we found on a rusty bike tossed into the gully. Mrs. Fundak was too fat to stand for more than a few minutes. When she tried, she teetered like a life-size Weeble.

"Good eating, boys?" she asked, her mouth full of Wonder Bread. Pete hung his head. His mouth moved over his sandwich mechanically.

"Yes, ma'am," I answered, taking pride in my manners.

The rolls of fat on Mrs. Fundak's face parted to reveal the glistening smile of a model. "You see," she said to Pete. "That's called politeness. That's called respect."

"May we be excused?" Pete asked.

"Now that's more like it." Mrs. Fundak nodded.

Outside, Pete kicked a frozen lizard against the trunk of a pine, waited for it to bounce back to his foot, then kicked it again. "I hate her," he said. "I mean, I really hate her."

"Hate is not an option," I said, repeating what my mother told me every time my father had left for work and failed to return. Secretly, I envied Pete's situation. Because his mother was so fat, she could rarely catch him to punish him, and since she couldn't drive, he'd been behind the wheel running her errands since he could see over the dashboard.

"Maybe she'll die," Pete considered. He lobbed the prostrate lizard across the front yard. "Dying is definitely an option."

• • •

By the time I arrived home, the sun was a yolky smear against a blanket of shapeless clouds. My mother: a bulge of snow beneath the benevolent arms of the mulberry tree. I found Lucie and Molly in the kitchen. Molly's placid face resting on the edge of the table like an expectant puppy.

"We're hungry," Lucie said, having long since spoken for Molly until we usually asked Lucie what Molly was thinking without addressing Molly at all.

The front door swung open, and there stood our mother, her dark hair white with snow. But her face flushed rosy and apple cheeked, as though she'd passed the day roasting by a fire. She held her hands in front of her, turned them over and then back again as if she'd gotten herself a new pair.

"It's the passion," she said, smiling at us, and when our mother smiled, even we recognized that she was beautiful by anyone's standards. "Do you understand what I am saying? He's lit a fire inside of me." Then she laughed, jubilant, until Lucie and I started laughing from her laughter.

Here's what Jesus said to our mother under the mulberry tree: *Paint that door. Make that door speak to those with closed hearts.*

She'd woken with the bed empty beside her, which wasn't unusual, but this time she'd found a note from our father that said something along the lines of "When I get famous I'll send money, don't forget to change the oil in the truck and have a good life." We weren't surprised. We'd found the note on her bedroom floor, had been expecting it for some time. But what we hadn't expected was our mother's reaction. She decided to get her ducks in a row, clean up ship, start afresh, and she chose to begin this new life by stripping and varnishing the front door (Rome wasn't built in a day, she reminded us), something she'd been asking our father to do for years. It was an important step, she explained. A sign of her independence. Only when she laid her hands on the door, she felt a surge of dizzying energy. That's when she heard Jesus for the first time: *Paint that door. Make that door speak to those with closed hearts.*

Jesus didn't mean with varnish, she was sure of that, but like a painting in a museum. And when she opened the door to day, she saw nothing but resplendent white, a new world, everything clean and erased, a blank canvas, and she believed.

"A door," our mother said, "is more than a door. So it makes sense. It's an opening and a closing. A beginning and an ending. A choice. He's standing at the door knocking. You see?"

She said all of this and more, then walked into her bedroom, shutting the door behind her.

Nothing was ever the same for us, as you'd expect.

• • •

The next day dawned surprisingly warm, the snow melted to mud, and we wondered aloud how anything so wondrous could have happened to the forgotten town of Edna.

Our mother packed us in the truck and drove two towns over to the art store, spent the week's grocery money on tiny tubes of paint she smeared into a heavenly world all over our old front door. When the paint ran out, she glued on buttons and scraps of fabric, things she'd been saving for years with no reason as to why.

"You see," she said, her hands layered in paint, "my whole life was preparation for this moment." Her eyes glazed filmy and feverish, and there was a kind of fire behind them that most people spend a lifetime searching for.

Here's what we thought: If only she'd make some black-eyed peas and macaroni and corn bread and banana pudding. But our mother didn't think about things like eating and bathing and cleaning after the day Jesus told her to paint that door. She said she was being fed by the hand of the Lord. Didn't we understand that?

It's hard to explain exactly what my mother painted onto those doors. Not anything with a name. Just an explosion of colors that filled you until a heat spread from your belly to your limbs to your fingertips and made you want to raise your hands to the spirit, and that's usually what happened. Believers from Tennessee and Georgia and Louisiana and sometimes farther started pilgrimaging to our house in expensive cars and pleated skirts and Sunday hats, dazed with bliss after laying their eyes upon the Lord's hand in my mother's work.

They left with a door strapped on top of their cars. Sometimes two. She couldn't make them fast enough. Locals hauled in truckloads of donated doors salvaged from old houses that rich people tore down. They brought paint and buckets of buttons and bundles of scrap fabric and anything shiny or precious that could be spared. My mother scraped the old lead paint off the doors, got them even and smooth as the quiet water my father loved to slice his boat into in the early hours of the morning, then painted herself ragged.

"The woman's done lost her mind," Pete's mother said when we wandered over for supper each evening, Molly tagged on Lucie's hip. "I'd call Social Services, but they'd probably just stick you in a home with some nutso who'd lock you in the basement."

The doors sold for more money than we'd ever seen. Lucie begged my mother to enroll her in the gifted school in Birmingham, begged her to send Molly to specialists. "Why?" my mother said. "What other book do you need besides the Bible? Why would Molly need to be anything other than what God made her?"

In those early days, whatever money my mother earned, she gave to Full Gospel Baptist. I know this is true, because nothing changed in our home. Not one new chair, not a dress for Lucie, not a toy for Molly.

• • •

Over a year later, in the midst of an unforgiving heat wave that kept Edna cooling itself in front of the few air conditioners in town, Bobby Alan Moon brought my mother his wisp of a daughter. "*Please,*" he pleaded with my mother. "*Help her.*"

My mother stopped painting, closed her eyes. "It has begun," she said.

But how could we have known?

The doctors in Mobile called Ray Moon "challenged." What the people of Edna said was, *She ain't right.* I guess it depends on how you look at it, but watching her standing in our door on that late June morning, her father pulling out of our driveway as fast as his car would take him, her pale arms clutching a shiny new Samsonite, I thought, Something is wrong here.

Ray had a condition. She'd been in a car wreck when she was just fourteen, less than a year before she turned up at our door, and something in her brain had died, the part that told right from wrong. According to my mother, that part shriveled like bad fruit and rotted away leaving room for the devil to fill and he did.

"Frontal lobe damage," Lucie said. "That's what's wrong with her. No impulse control. Nothing so dramatic as the devil."

None of us listened to Lucie. Our eyes were glued on Ray Moon.

She stood in our doorway for hours that first day, staring off into the distance, her fingers still wrapped around the handle of the suitcase. She wore a fine dress, lavender silk with black piping on the hem, and Lucie couldn't help but gawk, because the style was more suited to Lucie's age, and Lucie never had much and wanted all. Ray saw none of us. Her pale eyes: the color of smoke fading.

Lucie and I made dinner with limp vegetables Mrs. Fundak sent us. Lucie walked with a plateful over to Ray. She finally set down her suitcase, bending only at the waist. The heels of her black Mary Janes were punched together like a soldier's. She put her hands out for the plate but did not look at Lucie, and my sister, scared as a mouse, put the plate into Ray's outstretched hands.

"Thank you," Ray said, her first words to us. Her voice shocked us with its sweetness. She smelled of flowers, the scent overwhelming.

Ray's hands didn't so much let go of the plate as collapse. My mother's plate struck the floor, food splattering the linoleum and the hem of Ray's beautiful dress, and not a chip, not a sliver, came off that plate. It spun at her feet, whirring a thin sound, then stopped. "Why does he hate me?" she asked. "What have I done?"

"Take her and make her right," Bobby Alan Moon had said to my mother. "Fill her with whatever has filled you."

There is no cross you cannot bear. Ray Moon was ours.

We put Ray in Lucie and Molly's room, and they moved in with me, which made us irritable. We climbed over one another like crabs in a bucket. "You must be bigger than that," my mother said. "You must be strong."

For the first two days, Ray thrashed on Lucie's bed, still in her food-splattered dress, her long gold hair tangled over the pillow, her hands gouging her body, horrifying wails erupting from her throat. She wouldn't eat or speak or acknowledge us.

We fumbled through our days, drunk from the cloying smell of her. Lucie became sullen and listless, uninterested in her books. "Why bother?" she said.

Little Molly covered her ears every time Ray moaned or howled in agony. At the time, we were not aware of Molly's special kind of genius, didn't understand her hypersensitivity to loud sounds she could not control. She climbed from our bed in the night and hid in the shed. She slept curled around the garden tools. We found her there in the morning, tapping out elaborate rhythms on the blade of a shovel or ax.

"Let it be," our mother said about Ray. "We don't indulge spoiled children. She'll come around when she's wanting something."

Sure enough, the morning of the third day Ray sat up, taut backed and rigid, flipped her legs over the bed, grabbed her Samsonite suitcase from the closet, and locked herself in our only bathroom for several hours.

When she came out, her breasts wrapped in a scrap of purple fabric, her concave belly bare and glistening, a tiny black skirt low on her hips, her mouth as red and round as a fireball, I knew we were in for trouble.

"Why, hi," she said, looking straight at me. "Got anything to eat?" She smacked her lips the way old men do before Thanksgiving dinner.

"Gimme a break," Lucie said. She'd caught me staring at Ray's breasts. "Those ain't nothing but fat."

"Lucie," my mother said. "We don't speak of such things in this house." My mother stood in the kitchen, a paintbrush in each hand, blues dripping onto the floor. "Of course," she said to Ray, "you will have to change into something more appropriate."

Ray threw back her head, released a long, trebling keen. Then she shoved her hand down her skirt and began kneading wildly. "I hurt," she moaned.

"Oh, goodness," my mother said. "You have to stop that."

"I sure am hungry," Ray said.

My mother gave her one of my father's T-shirts to wear over her outfit and told me to take her over to Pete's house for some lunch. Mrs. Fundak made us a huge pot of macaroni and cheese with a block of cheddar melted on top.

Pete couldn't stop staring at Ray, kept whispering to me, "Look at the size of them tits." When Ray caught him looking, she blinked longingly.

"How old are you, girl?" Mrs. Fundak asked.

"Fifteen," Ray Moon said, cheddar cheese smeared on her chin. "This is good."

"What's that smell?" Pete said. He pushed his nostrils in the air.

"You're awful developed for fifteen," Mrs. Fundak said. "I mean, there ain't nothing wrong with that. But you should be careful. I was early developed, and it got me nothing but trouble." She sniggered. "Fun, but trouble."

"More," said Ray Moon, pushing her plate toward the bowl of coagulating pasta.

"It's not polite to ask for seconds in someone else's home," Mrs. Fundak said. "Look, Pete. You see how rude that is? Pete's not polite, either." Mrs. Fundak stared pointedly at Pete. "You see, boy? You see how ugly rude is?"

"May we be excused?" Pete said.

"Well," Mrs. Fundak said, rolling back a bit in her chair. "Now that's more like it."

We took Ray outside to show her the gully, and she immediately slid down its worn, dusty bank, squealing with pleasure the whole way, her skirt hiked up around her waist, her butt cheeks stained red from the dirt. There was something awe-inspiring in her lack of fear.

"I bet she'll do anything we tell her to," Pete said.

"You know why the dirt here is so red?" Ray yelled from the gully. "Iron. The soil is rich in iron. A lot of pregnant women like to eat it. That's called geophagy."

Pete looked at me, stunned. "I thought she was retarded," he said.

"Not all of her," I said. "Just the part that tells right and wrong."

"Well, hot damn," Pete said. "Hey, Ray," he yelled down the gully. "Take off your shirt and show us what you got."

Without hesitation, Ray pulled my father's white T-shirt over her head, then untied the purple scarf.

"Like this?" she said, radiant. Her breasts were as round and flawless as those in the dirty magazines we found on the side of the road near the Conoco, and I felt myself harden, no matter how much I willed my body to still.

"Oh, my God," Pete said. Then, "Do us a little dance."

Ray began pirouetting, her long, slender legs perfectly poised. She looked like she'd had some training.

"Watch this." Pete picked up a few pebbles, began pelting them at Ray as she twirled tornadoes of red dust.

"Ow!" Ray giggled. She rubbed her shoulder where a rock had hit her, gyrating her hips and humming the entire time.

I slapped the rocks out of Pete's hands. "What are you doing that for?" I said, knowing I should have said something sooner. "That ain't right."

Pete shrugged, kicked a clump of dirt over the edge of the gully, where it fell at Ray's dancing feet.

"Look around," he said. "There ain't much right."

• • •

My mother sent Ray to Bible school with the rest of us in July, but she was so disruptive—exposing herself in crafts class, putting her hands down her skirt during youth fellowship, letting boys fondle her breasts behind the juice machines at lunch—my mother was asked to withdraw her. She put Ray to prepping doors, and Ray chipped and sanded faithfully, the soft heart curve of her bottom peeking from under her skirt as she worked.

"Ray," my mother would say when she saw her pressing herself against some poor man there to get drunk in the spirit, "remember who you are. You are a child of God." We found Ray naked in the shed with more than one of the believers from Tennessee, Georgia, Louisiana, and sometimes farther.

"I've done something I shouldn't?" she'd say when my mother hauled her off the men and out of the shed. "I'm bad?" she'd ask. The men whimpered as if they'd been wronged, covered themselves with cupped hands.

For obvious reasons, my mother decided to keep Ray home when classes started in mid-August. After school, Ray and I sat on a bench in the front yard and talked. She told me about before the accident, how she'd been an honors student and a cheerleader, how she'd had an ant farm that won the science fair, how she'd won a ribbon at dance camp for the best line kicks, how a boy named Cameron kissed her for the first time at the sixth-grade homecoming dance.

I told her what I'd learned at school. How the core of the earth was partially made of iron, just like the red dirt pregnant women ate. Except the earth's core reached temperatures as high as 7,000 degrees Celsius, which was about the temperature of hell, I figured. How some nonbeliever scientists thought animals around us evolved from previously existing animals, that people could have been monkeys or amoebas once.

"Oh, I can believe that," Ray said. She leaned toward me confidentially, her hair tickling my forearm, her floral scent overwhelming. "When I was in that car wreck, I died for a few minutes. Like really dead. But I didn't see a tunnel of light or a bunch of angels in white robes like old people in church say. I was transformed into a bird with black-black wings that spread across a sky bluer than anything I'd ever imagined. And I flew. Just opened my wings and sailed across the world. Weightless. No pain. No worries. Just flight. It was amazing." Her smoky eyes filled with tears. "Sometimes, well . . . sometimes I wish they hadn't bothered bringing me back."

"You were knocked out," I told her. "You weren't a bird."

"Oh no," she said. "You better believe it. I was a bird." She gave my hand a friendly pat, left it there, and I wondered, not for the first time, what it said about me that a girl who couldn't control her sexual impulses with strange men somehow had none for me.

"In mythology, birds are powerful creatures," she said.

"How about fish?" I asked. "Are they powerful, too? Because if my father gets what he wants, in heaven he'll be a largemouth bass."

I could see my mother out of the corner of my eye, the melancholy stoop of her back as she bent over yet another door. I hadn't realized I was so angry.

"People can only give you what they have to give," Ray said softly. "Your mother, your father, my father, Pete, Mrs. Fundak. You just have to learn to accept what they can spare you."

"Is that what you do?" I said. "Take it when Pete *gives it to you*?" Immediately, I wanted to swallow my words. But there they were, boldfaced and obvious, my aching heart more responsibility than I could manage. I knew he came to her in the night; she didn't try to hide it. I watched them through my bedroom window, naked and intertwined in the soft grass beneath the mulberry tree.

Ray stood, regarded me coolly. "Now, there's no excuse for such hatefulness," she said finally. "You, of all people, have much more to offer."

And when she said it, I believed.

• • •

Under my mother's supervision, Ray seemed to be getting better. She quit rubbing herself at inappropriate times, stopped wailing and thrashing in her bed. Ray surprised everyone with memorization skills the doctors swore she would never recover, reciting long passages of scripture for my mother before bedtime.

"See," my mother said, pronouncing Ray practically cured. "The Word can do powerful things."

"Whatever," Lucie muttered. "God ain't got anything to do with it. Her brain's healing. That's called *nature.*"

And then, one morning Ray woke up and puked all over the fluffy green toilet cover.

"She's pregnant," Lucie said a little too gleefully. "And *that* is definitely nature."

"No," my mother said. "It's the evil working itself out of her. It's bound to make the girl ill." She didn't look convinced.

When I finally worked up the courage to tell Pete that he might be a father, I found Mrs. Fundak sitting alone in her special chair on the porch.

"He's gone," she said. "Not a note. Nothing. He always was a rude boy. Got it from his father." She looked like she hadn't bathed in days. She was dressed in a half-buttoned nightgown. Her hair clung to her scalp. "Who's going to roll my hair? Help me into the tub?" She slapped her fat thighs and sighed. Then she whirled her chair around and scooted back into the house on tiny, spidery feet.

A week later, Ray was running for the bathroom two or three times a day. If she wasn't puking, she curled up in bed, crying. When Lucie found Ray laid out cold on the bathroom floor, my mother rinsed off her paintbrushes and closed up shop. She packed us into the truck, then tore out to Full Gospel Baptist for counseling and prayer.

"I don't understand," Lucie said, scowling. "What's Preacher Willie going to do about a baby? Shouldn't we be going to a hospital?"

"It's not what Preacher Willie's going to do. It's what God wants us to do," my mother said.

"Preacher Willie ain't God," Lucie said.

"Shut up, Lucie." My mother's hands twitched uncontrollably on the steering wheel.

Over the recent months, thanks to my mother's donations, Preacher Willie had carpeted the sanctuary in a deep crimson, added a towering baptismal tank behind the altar, and a new glassed-in nursery in the foyer.

"The Lord has been good to us," said Preacher Willie. His entire office had been renovated—crimson carpet like the sanctuary, crimson velvet drapes, rose-colored stained-glass windows that tinged the room a milky red.

"It looks like the inside of God's belly," Lucie said. "Or maybe Jonah in the whale." My mother whacked the back of her head, smiled serenely at Preacher Willie.

"She'll have to get married," Preacher Willie said after my mother explained Ray's situation. He locked his watery eyes on Ray. She shuddered in the corner of the room. Her hands cradled her abdomen.

My mother stared blankly at Preacher Willie. She opened her mouth, but no sound came out.

• • •

That afternoon, my mother sat grimly at the kitchen table and flipped through the pages of her earmarked Bible, the doors, for once, forgotten. After a few hours, she slammed the Bible shut, tucked it under her arm, and marched into Ray's room.

For days, my mother sat at Ray's bedside, spooning special soups and teas into the girl's mouth. They clutched each other's hands, murmured low into the wee hours of the night. The sweet scent of Ray radiated from the room. The doors and windows were kept open day and night.

One morning, a loud shriek exploded from Ray's room. We heard glass breaking. Furniture being overturned.

"Here it comes," Lucie squealed.

"Here what comes?" I said.

"The baby, you idiot."

"What baby?" I asked.

Molly crawled into the corner.

"A baby takes nine months to make," I said.

"Not one you want to get rid of." Lucie slit her eyes narrow. "What do you think all them teas have been for?"

We peered into Ray's room. It looked as if a tornado had hit, knickknacks broken on the floor, the sheets slung from the bed, the nightstand on its side. And standing in the middle of the room with a writhing blanket in her hands was our mother.

Ray smiled at me. "I told you so," she said.

"If that's what a new baby's like," Lucie said, nodding at the thrashing blanket in our mother's hands, "I don't ever want to have me one."

"That's not a baby," my mother said, loosening the blanket so we could see. "It's a bird. It came in through the window and wouldn't go back out. I had a time catching it." And sure enough, you could just make out a long charcoal beak in the folds of the blanket, its shiny, darting eyes.

"Lovely, isn't it?" my mother said wistfully. "I've never touched a live one." She squatted on the floor next to Molly, who placed her hand tentatively against the stunned bird's inky black head.

"Bird," my mother said, enunciating slowly.

Molly chortled, patted the bird's head like a dog's. "Bird," she repeated, her first word, and we all stared at her in wonder. She smiled the same sad smile she was born with.

After everyone had a chance to stroke the bird, my mother walked reluctantly to the front door and opened the blanket. The bird lurched from her hands. In a matter of seconds, it was nothing more than a fluttering black gap against the day's sky.

"What about the baby?" Lucie said.

My mother held up a round gumball-size pebble with stony protruding spikes. It looked like something from my earth science book, a shrunken, undiscovered planet.

"That's what's left of the baby?" For once, Lucie looked confused.

"A kidney stone." My mother smiled. "The wounded soul is like any other living thing; it will push out rot sooner or later."

"Like your toe will push out a splinter left in too long?" I asked.

"Exactly," my mother said.

I peered into Ray's bedroom, where she leaned against a wall of pillows. The drapes billowed lazily in the morning breeze. Ray smiled tranquilly. "Did you see it, the bird?" She looked triumphant, as if something momentous about the mystery of the world had been revealed.

The next day, Bobby Ray Moon collected his daughter with little fanfare, as if he were picking her up from summer camp. He shoved a wad of bills in my mother's hand, and for once, perhaps understanding that she was worthy of better, my mother put the money in the bank instead of the collection plate at Full Gospel Baptist.

Time passed, as it will.

My mother saved enough money to move us to Birmingham, where her artwork was displayed in galleries to much critical acclaim. She enrolled Lucie in the gifted school, and my sister, who no longer felt like a freak, flourished. She eventually became a doctor and opened a clinic in Edna, where she felt she was needed most. My mother brought Molly a piano so she could put her twitching fingers to work, and although she's never spoken a complete sentence to this day, she tells epic stories with her music.

And eventually my shoulders broadened and my voice deepened and I became man enough to have my heart shattered soundly more than once, which is all we can ask for in life, those small moments of hope in the initial throes of love when all is still possible.

I never heard of Ray Moon again after the day she left our house wearing the same lavender dress in which she arrived. But I like to think she lives her life as fearlessly as that broken girl left on our doorstep, carrying with her, as do those who knew her one long-ago summer, the understanding that with faith, all that is lost and dark within us might somehow find a way to emerge into the inchoate world and take flight.

our former lives in art

"Beanie Weenies or Vienna sausages?" Peter says, pulling into the Texaco parking lot. He turns off the truck ignition, nudges his son's thigh for a response. In his camouflage shirt and new orange hunting vest, Fischer looks like any other country boy, and Peter thinks that maybe today will be a turning point, that maybe this is the beginning of something new between them.

Fischer stares at his sketchpad. Blinks.

"How about the Beanie Weenies? The lunch of champions. They've got fiber and protein. No way your mother can get bent out of shape about that, huh?"

"Sure," Fischer says. He turns his attention back to his sketchpad and begins whistling under his breath, a chronic habit. His hand moves over the paper in the uncanny way it does when he draws, like it doesn't belong to him.

"Beanie Weenies it is," Peter says. The forced enthusiasm embarrasses him, something he feels often when alone with his son. He looks at his watch. It's barely past one. He's supposed to entertain Fischer until four so Susie can get her nails done and do some shopping.

"You want anything else?" Peter says. He ruffles Fischer's hair. It hangs past his shoulders in pale ringlets, a style more fitting for a two-year-old than a second grader. Peter is waiting for the day Fischer gets his ass kicked at school, but Susie refuses to cut the boy's hair, perhaps because it is one of the few utterly childish things about him.

Fischer lifts his frail shoulders, tucks a curl behind his ears. Peter takes this for a no.

When Peter steps out of the truck, he shuts the door gently, not wanting to startle Fischer, who spooks easily at seemingly everyday things: a door closing, a car horn blaring, a dog barking in the distance.

Outside, the sky is the vast blue of an Alabama winter, and the cold of January fills his lungs. He feels his body relax. These are the kind of days that remind him why he's stayed in Millville all these years, even though he could make a lot more money in Atlanta, where idiots with money to burn pay top dollar for even the simplest jobs. Peter renovates old houses, mainly for wealthy northern transplants who like to wedge expensive plantation chairs on the verandas of their newly restored homes and pretend they live in a history that does not belong to them.

Millville is far-flung and sparsely populated, known for the lake vacationers flock to in the summer. Peter and Susie met when he was waiting tables at a seafood restaurant, one of those marina-type places on the lake where all the waiters have to dress like pirates. She came in with her sister for lunch, both of them in bikini tops and cutoff shorts, and Peter'd promised the hostess half his tips to seat them in his section.

Before Fischer was born, Peter and Susie sometimes camped at Wind Creek State Park, a tiny oasis on a finger of the lake. They would climb to the flat, granite cliffs slanting into water and make love, Susie pointing out the open field of a distant galaxy or far-off planets. Then they would simply lie there, silent at the weight of the world above them.

When Fischer was a toddler, they took him to Wind Creek. Peter wanted to teach him to swim, but his son screamed hysterically, as if the water burned. Peter put Fischer in a life jacket, walked to the end of the community pier, and plopped his son in the water. Hours later, when Fischer finally stopped crying, Susie called Peter an animal, looking at him for the first time the way she does so often now.

A few months later, Fischer found his art.

When Peter opens the door to the Texaco, the pungent smell of the bait kept in the tanks in the back reminds him of the summers of his childhood, and Peter wonders how much longer mom-and-pop places like this will be around. More and more, the country roads are peppered with the fancier stores, the kind where you can slip a credit card in the pump and never talk to an actual person.

The canned foods, covered in a thick layer of dust, are sandwiched between the toilet paper and the charcoal. Nothing looks like it's been touched since the Cold War era. Peter grabs two Beanie Weenies and some flat, wooden spoons from the box next to the ice-cream cooler. He thinks of getting a beer, but decides against it. Susie would freak if she knew he'd had a drink while handling guns around Fischer.

"Hi," the cashier says brightly when he goes to pay. She couldn't be more than sixteen, probably the owner's daughter, and she's wearing a tiny tank top even in this weather, the fabric stretched tight against her breasts. The local paper is spread over the counter. They don't print much real news in it, because there's not much real news to print in Millville, which is another plus for the town as far as Peter's concerned. But there's a whole section on local happenings—who spent the night with whom, where the Spanish class went for school break, whose house got rolled the weekend before, who got arrested for underage drinking—and the teens in the area compete to see who can get their name in the paper the most often. When Peter was a senior, he got a write-up for killing the buck with the widest rack that season, and he still has the clipping somewhere.

"Going hunting?" the girl says, nodding at Peter's orange cap.

"Just skeet shooting. It's my son's first time." He looks over her shoulder to make sure Fischer is still in the truck, and spots him huffing on the passenger window, drawing in the condensation left behind. Peter doesn't need to see to know that his son is drawing a row of cannons.

"Any pertinent news?" Peter says. He tries not to stare at the girl's breasts.

"Huh?" The girl moves to ring up his purchases at a glacial speed.

"The newspaper."

"Oh," she says, smiling. "Just this old dude that died behind some diner on a business trip to St. Louis. He went to pee behind the diner and slipped into the river. They think he was drunk or something. He couldn't pull himself out."

Peter looks at the picture of the dead man in the paper, and it takes him a moment to recognize the face of Richard Watson, a boy he went to high school with. They used to go bird hunting with a group of friends. To be honest, Peter had forgotten that Richard Watson existed until just this moment. He feels embarrassed then frightened that a person could forget someone he once knew.

"Two kids and a wife," the girl says. "Isn't it amazing." She snaps her silver-ringed fingers. "*Bam.* Just like that, and it's all over."

When Peter gets back to the truck, Fischer has finished with the window, and is back to sketching in his pad.

Another battle scene. The central focus: a gutted Confederate attempting to reinsert his intestines into the open cavern of his belly.

Fischer's first word was "art," and he'd said it like he meant it. Then, "my art, my art," a constant wail until Susie shoved a set of fingerpaints his way, and his pudgy fingers exploded into color. In an hour he offered up, on a paper grocery bag, a perfect cannon, a Brooke rifled cannon they would learn later, properly shaded and proportioned, a weapon neither of his parents had ever seen. He was not yet three.

That day, Peter and Susie sat hand in hand next to Fischer, watching him paint, the terror that passed between them unspoken.

"Perhaps it's hereditary, something from your dad," Susie said after Fischer fell asleep, a dozen paintings of meticulously rendered cannons clutched to his chest. He'd refused to go to bed without them.

"Art," Peter's own father had often said, "is not always kind, or easy."

Peter's father had been a forensic artist for the state. Sometimes he would sketch the faces of decomposed Jane and John Does found in the alleys, forest, Dumpsters, but of course, he sketched them how they once looked, alive, using their bone structure, approximate age, probable race, in hopes that loved ones would recognize the images and claim the remains. Peter, encouraged by his mother, who hated the violence his father's work brought into their home, went the way of normal boys. He took up hunting and fishing and football, then beer and women, then a wife, a kid, a job—the real kind.

"Hereditary?" Peter said. "My father didn't even own guns, let alone a fucking cannon. A *cannon,* Susie."

There's no way they could have known how bad it would get.

Over the last four years, Fischer has drawn the same figures repeatedly, their faces moribund and hollow-cheeked. The drawings are gruesome. Soldiers' bones jutting from flesh. Limbless men submerged in murky ravines. But the landscape in which these brutal deaths take place is rendered with frightening sensitivity to detail, and one cannot ignore their beauty.

Peter puts the cans of Beanie Weenies on the dashboard, waits for Fischer to acknowledge his presence.

"Twentieth Maine and Fifteenth Alabama," Fischer says without being asked. He just lost his front teeth, and his th's sound like f's.

"How do you know?" Peter says. "I mean a soldier's a soldier, right?"

"I just do." When Fischer raises his head to answer, Peter is struck silent by his son's haunting beauty—the vein-mapped skin, the clarity of the pale, sober eyes. Peter is reminded of the *memento mori* daguerreotypes they'd seen at the National Archives last fall, a trip Susie planned that did nothing but encourage Fischer's obsession in Peter's mind. The children in the photos were impossibly pallid, some of them with their eyes still open, their gazes glassy and vacant. When the archivist explained that *memento mori* means "remember your death" in Latin, Peter told Susie he had to go to the bathroom. Instead, he walked the ten blocks back to the hotel and sat in the bar and got good and soused before Susie found him for the inevitable fight.

"Here, eat," Peter says, pulling off the top of one of the cans and shoving it toward Fischer. "And don't cut yourself."

"I'm not hungry."

"I didn't ask you if you were hungry." Peter pokes an ice cream spoon in Fischer's can, then grabs the sketchbook and sticks it in the glove compartment.

• • •

They sit in the truck for a while at the shooting range, watch waves of blackbirds roll from one oak into the next.

Peter finds himself growing increasingly maudlin over Richard Watson's death, a hazy kind of sadness that he suspects has more to do with him than his old friend. Two kids, he thinks. A widow. Damn.

He eyes Fischer, his face as placid as unrippled water, and wonders what it would take to evoke some type of honest emotion from his son. Peter imagines his own death. Maybe in a nasty car wreck. Or an accident at one of his work sites. This is a game he plays often with himself. He thinks of various tragic demises for himself, and then he pictures Susie and Fischer standing over his casket at the funeral. Sometimes Fischer clutches his mother's legs and wails. Other times he throws himself on his father's coffin. No matter the scenario, Fischer always responds with enthusiastic grief. Peter knows it's perverse, but he finds the images comforting.

"You ready?" Peter says. "You'll be an expert shot in no time."

Peter half expects Fischer, who's drawn enough guns to arm a brigade, to whip the Stevens 311 out of his hands and handle it like a veteran. But Fischer won't touch the gun when Peter tries to explain how to load it properly. He won't even pull the release string on the skeet thrower.

"Can we go to the art store now?" Fischer says within five minutes. His voice quivers. Peter tries not to resent it.

"We'll go to Wal-Mart later and you can pick out anything you want. But just try this first, okay? It took me months to convince your mother to let you shoot with me, and who knows when she'll let us go again. We'll practice without the skeet first. Maybe that will be easier."

Peter lifts the Stevens to his shoulder, aims at an imaginary quail, then shoots into the sky, the butt of the gun kicking into his flesh in a familiar way.

"See," he says, eyeing where the shot went without removing the Stevens from his shoulder, "since this is a double barrel, we don't have to reload, just pull the second trigger."

When Fischer doesn't respond, Peter turns to see the boy sitting on the ground, his hands over his ears. Peter clicks on the safety, swings it under his arm, kneels beside Fischer.

"There's nothing to be scared of," he says. "It's loud, that's all. The recoil's nothing but a love tap."

But Fischer won't get up, and the more Peter tries to persuade him, the more he resists, until Peter is talking much louder than he wants. Fischer buries his head between his knees.

Peter just intends to massage the boy's shoulders, to help him relax, but when his hands make contact with Fischer, the boy flinches as if he's been hit. Peter grabs Fischer by the back of his vest, lifts him to his feet, thrusts the gun in his hand, crouches behind him, places the shotgun against his son's shoulder, flips the safety off, wraps his son's finger around the trigger with his on top, and aims at the sky. In the midst of Fischer's screams, Peter pulls the trigger. The kick slams his son's torso into his chest.

Fischer howls. Someone yells, "Everything all right?" Peter feels his pulse in his throat.

"If you hold the gun too loose to your shoulder, like we just did," Peter explains, "it'll kick like a mule. So next time, hold it firm."

Fischer grips his shoulder, his bottom lip wedged between his teeth. His eyes film with tears.

"Get in the truck," Peter says. "If you're going to ruin it, just get in the truck."

Fischer runs to the truck and throws himself into the cab. Peter slumps onto the tailgate.

"Everything all right?" a voice says again. Peter looks up to see a tall, silver-haired man in an orange sweatshirt and overalls, a shotgun cradled to his chest. Behind him, a gawky teenage girl in an orange hunting cap that says DIVA across the bill kicks at the red dirt with her booted feet, her gangly legs as thin as the barrel of her Remington.

"Just first-time jitters."

"Are you sure?" the man says. "He doesn't seem so good."

Peter turns to see Fischer, partially obscured by the empty gun rack, kneeling in the seat, drawing on the rear window. His face is ashen.

A gust of wind blasts from the east; red dirt orbits their boots in small, opaque clouds. "He's just overly sensitive," Peter says. He can taste the iron-rich dirt in his mouth.

The man's expression remains uncertain, the same expression of doubt and disapproval Peter recognizes on the faces of Fischer's teachers when they see his artwork, the unspoken accusation: *What have you done to your child?*

• • •

It has been months since Susie has had any time for herself, and by the time Peter and Fischer get home, she's in an unusually good mood. When Peter bends to kiss her, she offers her mouth instead of her cheek. They open a couple of bottles of wine and make hamburgers for an early dinner. The few times Fischer speaks, Peter half expects him to blurt out the day's events, to sabotage the fragile truce in the house; but Fischer draws in his sketchpad, eats his dinner, then goes to bed without protest. When Susie asks about the day, Fischer doesn't mention the shooting range. He simply shows her his new sketch, and she tacks it on the wall, already cluttered with scores of similar sketches.

Susie insists on hanging up all of Fischer's artwork. When Peter opens the refrigerator for a sandwich or beer after work, haggard soldiers lurch at him with their bayonets. When he walks down the hall, rows of cannons careen at his head.

The few times they've invited company over, Peter could not persuade Susie to take down the drawings. Instead, she shows them off with the passion of a Little League mom. Susie never seems to notice that although their friends and family are awed by Fischer's drawings, they often ignore the child who produced them or eye him suspiciously, as if he knows something of their own bodies' betrayals, their tendency to decay.

"I had some time to think today," Susie says as they settle into bed. Her feet are ice-cold against Peter's calves.

He nuzzles her neck, says, "No thinking. Just feeling." He drags a thumb across her nipple, feels it harden in response. But her body doesn't relax, and she doesn't lean into him. Peter has quit counting the weeks since they've made love.

"I'm serious," she says, pushing him away. "I want to take Fischer to see Dr. Stevens again. We agreed that if the drawings didn't stop, we'd give it another chance."

"No," Peter says. He sits up and turns on the lamp. Susie has the covers pulled over her chin, and he yanks them off so he can see her face. "Discussion over. Let's don't start this one again."

After Fischer drew his first violent battle scene, eviscerated soldiers and all, Peter and Susie panicked. They eyed each other warily, both suspecting that the other one was damaging Fischer in some way, that surely the boy had to be suffering severe abuse to create such horrific images.

Finally, they took him to a psychiatrist. Peter thought the

doctor would prescribe a pill or two—hell, half of Fischer's preschool class was medicated—and that would be the end of it.

They picked Dr. Stevens out of the Auburn phone book, too embarrassed to ask anyone for a recommendation. Peter disliked her immediately. She was one of those plain, arrogant women who arm themselves with degrees when they realize their looks won't get them anywhere. She enunciated her words slowly when speaking to them, as if they were idiots, even though Peter has a couple of degrees himself. She touched his arm when he shifted uncomfortably, which was often. But they were desperate, and after a couple of sessions, she convinced them to allow her to use regressive hypnosis.

"Clearly," she said afterward, "it's a past life." She said this as if it were the flu, tonsillitis.

"Clearly," Peter said on the drive home, "she's a moron."

According to Dr. Stevens, under hypnosis Fischer gave all kinds of details about his supposed past life: Over 160 years ago a man named Wilton or Wilson or William was born on a small plantation somewhere east of Millville, Alabama. He had at least three older sisters, she said, one of whom died of some type of brain ailment, most likely cancer. His mother died before he was old enough to remember her. He had a saddlebred, and he loved it like a childhood friend. When he returned from the war in late 1865, he used to sketch his memories by the quiet of a creek on the east end of his property. Before he died, he placed his sketches in a pile and burned them. His father grew cotton, owned slaves before the war, but was a generous man, wise, jovial, and he whistled all the time. He'd left with his son in '61, but never made it home. When Wilton or Wilson or

William was in his late thirties or early forties, he eased himself one winter night, nude, into the cold waters of the creek and waited. For what, no one knows. One of his sisters found him, dazed and frostbitten, and took him inside. She tucked him into his boyhood bed, a view of a great oak out his window, and sat with him while he died, sometimes singing a song, something about Jesus or heaven or grace.

"The woman's a nutcase," Peter says. "I don't want her putting ideas in his head."

"Would it be so bad to have a special son?" Susie says. "A miracle son, even. A gift from God." The tone of her voice is hopeful, and Peter understands that Susie is tired, that she needs a name for what her son is, and "miracle" or "gift" is better than the alternatives.

As far as Peter's concerned, he would rather remain unknown to a God who would give a boy life only to make him spend it reliving a blighted past.

"My lawyer says I can petition a judge to order that Fischer get psychiatric help."

"Your lawyer?" Peter says. "Since when do you have a lawyer? Is that where you went today? I thought you were getting your nails done."

"I did that, too."

"Do you ever wish he was just gone?" Peter says finally. "I mean, not dead in some horrible way, just not here, with us." The words fall out of his mouth.

Susie lifts herself onto her elbows, pushes her short hair off her forehead. In the low light of the bedside lamp, she looks almost like the girl he met over a decade ago, and he wants to press his lips against the lobe of her ear, the sharp edge of her shoulder blade, but he knows it would be a performance of sorts, a mimicking of familiar gestures that had long ago lost their meaning.

"The day I met you at the restaurant, when you were wearing that dumb pirate outfit," Susie says, "I left my number as a joke. My sister bet me that I wouldn't do it. When you called and asked me out, I went because I didn't know how to say no. My whole life changed over a stupid bet."

"Maybe that's just how life happens," Peter says. "Look at my friend Richard Watson."

Susie turns sharply toward him. The hollows under her cheeks are deep and pronounced. She looks old.

"Who the fuck is Richard Watson?"

"We used to hunt together when we were teenagers," Peter says. "He died. Drowned in the river in St. Louis a few weeks ago. Apparently, he got drunk and went to take a piss behind a diner, fell into the river, and couldn't pull himself out. A wife and two kids. I saw it today in the paper."

"His wife must be so proud." Susie stares at him pointedly. Peter wonders, not for the first time, when his own wife forgot how to forgive.

"Besides," she says, "I don't give a damn about Richard Watson. We're talking about our son."

"You're drunk," Peter says. "You only cuss like this when you're drunk."

"You know," Susie says, "I read the other day that the majority of couples who lose a child divorce."

"What's that got to do with anything?"

"That's what you act like, as if Fischer were dead."

Outside, the rain plucks steadily on the copper roof Peter was so pleased with when he'd finished the restoration of their home.

"Perfectly authentic," he'd said to Susie the night Fischer was conceived, and she had gazed contentedly from where she hovered above him, naked and splendid as the ancient moon that lit them.

• • •

When Susie finally falls asleep, Peter slips from the bed and puts on his robe. He feels his way to the kitchen in the dark. His tongue sticks to the roof of his mouth, dry from the dark wine, and he's drinking his third glass of water before he looks out the window and sees Fischer, wearing nothing but his footed Batman pajamas, sitting on the concrete of the back patio. This isn't entirely unusual. Since Fischer began walking, he would intuitively unlatch the locks on the doors and wander around the yard. Susie had wept from exhaustion. It took them months to break him of the habit.

Peter eases open the sliding glass doors and walks toward Fischer. For a moment, he stands there watching his son, who stares into the distance.

He squats next to Fischer, places a palm against the boy's narrow back. He can feel the fragile knitting of bones that cradle his son's heart. Peter thinks of the pictures his father brought home for work, the gawking skulls, the delicate fissures where the bones meet, how vulnerable we look stripped of flesh, laid bare.

"You want to tell me what you're doing?"

"I'm hearing the quiet," Fischer says.

The tree limbs moan with the winter winds, and occasionally, Peter can hear the rush of a car winding down the county road.

"It's not very quiet," Peter says.

"It's louder in here." Fischer raps his knuckles hard against his forehead. Peter grabs his son's hand before he can do it again, his fingers shivering with fear or cold. How, Peter wonders, could he have not protected Fischer from this?

"C'mon," Peter says, reaching under the boy's arms to pull him up to standing. "I want to show you something."

• • •

Peter's latest renovation project is an old plantation house near Auburn, just a few miles from the university. It was built in 1850 using timber from the fifty or so acres on which it sat. The man who built it named it Greenland, and it stayed in the family until the year before, when his great-great-grandson died, the last of the line. A restaurateur from Birmingham bought it with the intent to turn it into a reception hall for parties and weddings, a dollhouse for the doe-eyed coeds spilling out of college and into matrimony. One-hundred-and-fifty-year-old English boxwoods lined the drive, and a constellation of cedar trees and giant hollies exploded from the lawn, shading the wraparound porch.

The house and its grounds will be finished by May in time for wedding season, and for some reason it breaks Peter's heart, the idea of clueless college kids who can't appreciate the architecture dancing on its original hardwood floors to "Mustang Sally" or "Brick House," the girls' high heels dangling from their wrists like limp corsages.

To compensate for the wine, Peter drives slowly on the way to Greenland. He knows these roads well, cruised them with teenage girlfriends, girls he could have easily ended up with instead of Susie. Then Fischer came, and everything that had been familiar in his life vanished. Now, winding through the quiet of the dark night, he can't help but wonder whose life he is leading.

Peter thinks of Richard Watson. His memories of Richard from high school are illusory and fragmented, small flashes like from a movie seen long ago: Richard waving from his father's yellow Corvette, his smile cocky and sure; Richard dancing in his boxers at a party, an empty beer case on his head; Richard lying beneath the tree stand from which they hunted deer, daydreaming aloud about the naked body of a girl whose name Peter has long forgotten.

What had Richard experienced, standing behind that diner in St. Louis, thinking he was going to take a piss and go back inside to his coffee, his hash browns? What choices led him there, to that moment? Did he have any time after he slipped into the Mississippi to examine his life and feel content in any small way, as if something were completed? Does anyone? Or maybe he just laid himself back into the water and gave himself over with great relief, much like Wilton or Wilson or William, watching the night watch him.

Fischer fell asleep during the ride, and Peter parks the truck near the front porch before waking him.

"What do you think?" Peter says, nudging Fischer as he

turns on the brights. The house is magnificent in the flood of light, a ghost from another time.

"Well," Peter says, "does it remind you of anything?" If this is what it was going to take to connect with his son, he was willing to try.

"What?" Fischer says, confused.

"You know, does it remind you of anything you've seen before? I mean, not this house exactly, but one like it. The one you talked about with Dr. Stevens."

"Oh," Fischer says. He looks at his feet.

"Do you want to go in and see if that helps?"

"No," Fischer says. His lack of enthusiasm angers Peter, and suddenly the whole endeavor feels foolish. Did he think they would share cigars and sip brandy on the veranda while Fischer shared war memories from the old days?

"Get your ass out of the truck," Peter says.

Fischer stares at him, timorous and silent. When Fischer gets out of the truck and walks to the steps of the porch, hunched and shivering, his face spectral in the headlights, Peter doesn't move to follow. The truck is still in drive, which Peter knows is stupid and dangerous. But what if? What if his foot slipped? What if he just meant to drive away for a moment to teach the boy a lesson, and his boot got caught on the gas pedal, and Fischer, stunned in the glare of headlights, didn't move fast enough? If Peter read such a thing in the paper, he would believe it. A tragic accident, no different from Richard Watson slipping into a roiling river behind a Waffle House.

But watching his son tremble in the cold, not speaking, not crying out for his father to come to him, Peter knows that what devastates him is not that he doesn't want Fischer for a son, but that Fischer might not want him for a father. And wasn't this the age-old story of fathers and sons? Peter wanted a father with a normal job at the mill, one who talked about football scores and admired the curve of a woman's breast without imagining the bone that lay beneath it.

"C'mon," Peter says, "get in the truck."

Fischer sprints toward the passenger door, his pajama feet slapping the ground as he runs.

"I'm not mad at you," Peter says after Fischer gets in the truck. He can see his breath whirl in the frigid air as he speaks, as if his words are tangible things.

"I'm cold," Fischer says. Peter grabs an old wool blanket from behind the seat, arranges it around the boy's shoulders.

"There's a horse around back," Peter says.

"A saddlebred?"

"Maybe." Peter puts the truck in reverse and backs away from the house, circling around the added-on garage. He stops in front of a tiny pond behind a long white fence. In the distance, there is the shadowy figure of a horse grazing. Peter turns off the headlights so they don't startle it.

"Its neck's too short," Fischer says, disappointed. "Saddlebreds have nice long necks."

The horse seems to float across the field, its body a shade darker than the night it moves through.

"You reckon he's lonely out there by himself?"

Fischer doesn't answer. He's already asleep, his eyes twitching under the thin skin of his lids, his hair tawny even in the absence of light. Peter knows from the research Susie unearthed that if this small boy in footed pajamas were actually part of the 15th Alabama, at this time in 1863, he would be in northern

Virginia, more than likely sick, definitely starved, waiting for promised action that would be a long time in coming, maybe staring at a night much like this one.

Peter is reluctant to leave Greenland. Susie will probably be up, frantic, and whether he is ready or not, once he calms her down, decisions will have to be made. But for now, he feels a sense of calm with his son silent beside him. He tugs part of the blanket, warm from Fischer's body, over his chest, then reclines his seat so he can get an unobstructed view of the sky through the side window.

Lightning marbles the night, electric gold against black, and then nothing. No distant galaxies. No far-off planets. Just blackness. If Peter didn't know better, he might believe that nothing exists in the universe except him and Fischer, this one present moment. He thinks of the earth's endless spinning, its inevitable motion of return, and he is strangely comforted by how negligible their lives must be for them to feel so still in the midst of such great movement.

acknowledgments

So many people have assisted me in the writing of these stories, and I am grateful to all of them. I owe a great debt to my family for their support and patience. Ryan Jurkovic kept me sane through the birth of these stories, and his tender humor was a much needed lifeline. A special thanks to my dearest friends, readers, and fellow writers, Shannon McCreery Lewis and Carolyn Hembree. Julia Cheiffetz, my editor at Random House, worked on these stories tirelessly. Her insight was greatly appreciated. And finally, thank you to my agent and advocate, Jin Auh, who always maintained faith in my work.

I would also like to acknowledge the Djerassi Resident Artist Program and the Washington Artist Trust for their generous support.

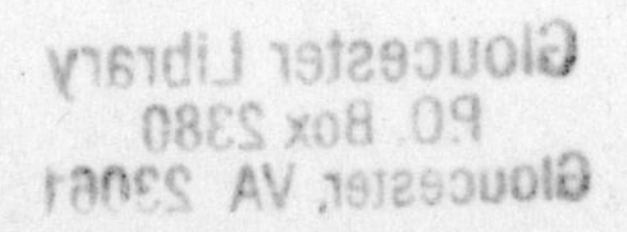

PHOTO: © LUCY DARE

JENNIFER S. DAVIS is the author of *Her Kind of Want,* which won the 2002 Iowa Award for Short Fiction. Her fiction has appeared in *Grand Street,* the *Oxford American, The Paris Review,* and *One Story.* She lives in Denver, Colorado.